# ALLIGATOR SWEATPANTS

Shawn Baker + Kev Nivek

# DEDICATIONS

*To My Late-Father and John Lennon.*

*I'm just sitting here watching the wheels go round and round,*
*I really love to watch them roll.*
*No longer riding on the merry-go-round,*
*I just had to let it go.*

-Shawn Baker


*For my Mother, Father, and my Beloved Baby Brother.*

*Your undying support has been a light in the darkness, a constant reminder of what is most important. I hope to someday repay you for all the blessings you have brought into my life.*

-Kev Nivek

# CONTENTS

# COMPANY TIME
## BY KEV NIVEK

The pain shot through him like a punch to the gut. He keeled over with a groan as the once dull and consistent pain had crescendoed into one as sharp as a chef's knife. Ted rested his head on the drab desk in his cubicle. Sweat caused his forehead to slide atop it with each new convulsion brought forth from the depths of his bowels.

*GRRRRAAACCCNNNHHHHHH*

He slammed his hands on the desk and clenched his muscles together, desperately attempting to hold himself together as another life-altering cramp shot through his intestines.

*GRRROOUUUONCCCHHHHH*

"Fuck this." Ted tried jumping to his feet but quickly resorted to grabbing the back of his desk chair, leaning on it as another cramp took hold. Making his way to the hall, he leaned against the walls of his coworker's cubes in order to stay on his feet.

Stumbling out of his department near the security guard's station in the center of the third floor, Ted managed a weak grin and wave as the overtly friendly guard saluted from his post, grinning to himself over a half-finished crossword.

"Hey, Taz! Nice to see ya." Ted muttered under his breath as he limped past the guards' station to the bathroom door in the hallway. As he reached the shallow hall, Ted saw two of his coworkers heading into the bathroom.

Fear gripped him as his stomach let out a meek gurgle.

Composing himself as he pushed through the door, Ted's fears were realized. He gazed blankly for a moment at the two shut stalls. The sounds of zippers opening and belts hitting the tile let him know he'd have some minutes to wait.

Cursing quietly, he waddled back to the hall as sweat rolled down his brow. Lurching forward, he rested both hands on the water fountain that sat on the wall between the two restrooms. Leaning in, he let the cool water run over his barely open lips. Ted was afraid to drink it.

Another bout of intense pain shot through him, accompanied by a symphony of bubbling stomach acid. Pushing away from the fountain, he leaned back against the wall opposite the entrance.

"Come on, come *on*, dammit." The cramps intensified, forcing Ted to double over—with his head between his knees as he tried desperately to hold in the grunts of pain. However, he should've been focusing on holding something else in...

*BUUURRRAAAAAPPPPSSSHH*

Eyes bulging, he perked up as much as his contorted abdomen would allow. Clenching as hard as possible, he began to limp back the way he had come, pushing past the security post to the elevators in the third-floor lobby.

Rapidly pressing on the call button to head down, Ted pounded it over and over again—hoping to will the lift up to him. Looking up, his eyes met those of Taz, who was staring quizzically at him through the guard post window.

*DING

With a startled hop, Ted turned back to face the elevator door. Rocking back and forth, he shot forward as soon as the doors opened, unwittingly slamming into poor Miss Beverly, the lovely head of accounting.

"Ope!" He reared back with a pivot. "So sorry, Miss Bev. . .didn't see you there."

"Hmph. I noticed," she said with a chuckle, shaking her head while walking through the glass doors onto the sales floor.

Ted dove into the elevator, pummeling the button to the second floor. After an arduous wait, the old box creaked to a halt as the door crept open. Wiggling through the still-opening door, he tore down the hallway to the second-floor men's room.

Ted's heart sank as he reached the end of the hall. Turning the corner, he could hear the unmistakable sounds of the cleaning crew.

Eyes shut and fingers crossed, he offered up a prayer.

*Please, God, be mopping the women's room. . .*

Ted stopped dead in his tracks as God responded with a sign.

CLOSED FOR CLEANING

"Are you fucking shitting me?!"

The unintended pun was met with another awkward squawk from below. His only solace was the door directly across the hall from him. The elevator felt miles away, but the first-floor bathroom was right next to the stairway.

Scooting, Ted resembled Quasimoto as he ducked into the stairwell.

The stairs proved to be an unusual challenge; and after shuffling down the first half of the flight, he found himself practically sliding down the rail for the final few steps.

Ted stumble-slid off the rail, slamming into the brick wall at the base of the steps. Leaning heavily on the wall, he dragged himself to the door. He took three deep breaths before he was forced into motion by another guttural warning shot.

*Grrrrrooouuuunch*

Sweat was running down his temples as he reached for the door. Heaving with all of his might, he swung the heavy wooden door open as he lunged through it, crashing helplessly into an unsuspecting Melanie.

*AAAAGGHHH!!*

The adorable saleswoman shrieked as her carryout soup flew from her hands, showering Ted on its way to the floor.

"Jesus, Ted. What the fuck's wrong with you!?" she screamed at him as he fell backward, virtually crab-walking away on his quest to quell the storm raging inside him.

"I'm really sorry, Mel." He wiped sweat and cheddar broccoli from his upper lip while cautiously shuffling away. "I'm so sorry."

Turning, he tore down the hallway, salvation a mere fifteen feet away.

The light dimmed at the end of the tunnel as he noticed a young man walking a few feet ahead of him. He swallowed his fear with an audible gulp.

*Hhhrrraaaaoooonnnckkk*

Another intense cramp froze him in his tracks momentarily. His heart skipped a beat as he saw the young man entering the men's room. Ted started to call out to the man but stopped when he saw the headphones attached to his ears.

Ted hobbled his way to the door, shouldering through it with his momenta. He slid on the wet tile floor, grabbing onto the sink to keep from falling. Hardly composed, he looked up from his feet.

There it was—in all its glory.

The stall door to his left hung open. Ted wasted no time.

Sliding into the small stall, he faintly heard the rhythmic bassline through his stall mate's earbuds. He paid it no mind as he slammed the lock shut.

*GRRRROUAAAAAACCCHHKK*

Ted's whole body clenched as he frantically fumbled with his belt, finally unfastening his soup-lathered dress pants.

The explosion occurred before Ted even felt the cold porcelain beneath him. What followed was a moment of pain and euphoria, something like that of a sneeze. Only this particular sneeze would last twenty minutes. Or was it three hours? No matter. Time was no longer present as his entire system unceremoniously evacuated itself.

The embarrassing sounds and smells horrified him. A courtesy flush was quickly followed by a new round of blasphemy.

Once the dust had settled, Ted sat a moment, sweating profusely with his pointy elbows on his bony knees. With one supreme sigh, he leaned forward while reaching for the tissue paper.

Ted's heart stopped as his fingers touched the rigid cardboard of an empty roll.

# PLACE OF WORSHIP
## BY SHAWN BAKER

The moonlight shone through the stained glass windows and lit up the rosewood pews, creating a natural light throughout the nave. Greg and Dino sat in silence, passing the communion wine bottle back and forth. They savored every gulp as it slid down their throats, leaving a bitter grape aftertaste.

The two men sat in the first row, admiring the decor. Christmas was less than a week away and the church interior reflected the season. There were six Christmas trees, three on each side of the altar, draped with lights from top to bottom. The altar table was covered with a gold cloth, lined with purple garlands and six candles placed across the top. Poinsettias rested along the edge of the altar, just above the steps. The giant crucifix that hung above it all, developed a luminous glow from the lights on the trees. The whole arrangement was just breathtaking.

"Yo, Dino. . ." a bewildered Greg began as he stared at the altar.

"Yeah?" Dino replied, also fixated on the decorations.

"Think we're going to hell for this shit?" Greg asked.

"Um. For what?"

"You know. . .for breaking into this church...stealing the wine. . .and like. . .breaking into the church."

"Hell no, man. First of all, we didn't STEAL anything! We have the right to drink this wine just as much as the next slapdick that walks through those doors. If anything, those government bastards are the ones who are guilty of theft. They STOLE our right to drink when they passed that sorry ass law re-prohibiting the sale of alcohol. It ain't our fault that churches are the only ones who have legal access to the stuff. Shit, I bet you the overseer has plenty of booze to drink. So no, I don't think we're going to hell. We did nothing wrong. Since when was the pursuit of happiness wrong? Huh? Tell me."

Now facing Dino eye to eye, Greg was stunned. He didn't know whether to agree with Dino's reasoning or to object. Either way, he was buzzing from the wine and couldn't care less if he burned in hell or not.

"Well...fuck it," Greg finally retorted.

"Amen, brotha—*amen!*" replied Dino as he took another big swig from the bottle.

Dino passed the bottle to Greg and stood up in an attempt to stretch, but was brought back to his seat abruptly as his legs buckled from underneath.

"Holy shit man, you okay?"

Dino sat there quietly, his eyes widened as if he'd seen a ghost. Greg reached out to put a hand on his shoulder. Dino's body was stiffer than a new pair of shoes. His skin became pale as he started to convulse.

"DINO! Talk to. . .me," muttered Greg as his jaw tightened and his vision blurred.

Greg watched helplessly as his friend shook and moaned in agony. Dino took one final breath before becoming motionless. Greg's chest tightened as he fell to the floor, shattering the wine bottle he held in his hand. Lying face-forward on the concrete, and unable to move, Greg heard footsteps echoing in the distance.

As the sound of movement grew closer, Greg began to choke on his own blood. Greg was then flipped onto his back by the foot of another man. It was a face he had never seen before. This man stood tall, dressed in all black with the exception of a white clerical collar.

"For the flesh sets its desire against the Spirit, and the Spirit against the flesh; for these are in opposition to one another, so that you may not do the things that you please," said the priest as he hovered over Greg, staring into the windows of Greg's soul as he continued to speak scripture. "Then the LORD saw that the wickedness of man was great on the earth, and that every intent of the thoughts of his heart was only evil—continually."

Greg bellowed in pain as he coughed up blood that landed on the priest. Remaining stone-faced and unfazed, the man proceeded with his unwanted sermon. "Indeed, there is not a righteous man on earth who continually does good and who never sins. That is Ecclesiastes 7:20, my favorite scripture. Perhaps the most relatable of them all!"

Greg gazed at the priest with rage in his eyes, unable to speak back. He wanted nothing more than to be able to tell this man to go fuck himself.

"You see, no man is free of sin. . .myself included. I never intended on you and your friend to drink the wine I had prepared for my congregation. That was made specially for them. That wine was meant to wash away the wickedness that fills the souls of the members of this church. Not one person who walks through those doors for Mass truly wants forgiveness. None of them are truly apologetic for their evil ways. How can you be forgiven when you don't even believe you are wrong? It's too bad your friend isn't here to answer that question. I'm sure he'd have MUCH to say on this topic."

Pausing from his rant, the priest looked over at Dino's lifeless body. Greg lied there, animosity pumping through his veins. As he felt the force of death creeping upon him, he used every last bit of energy he had left to try and mumble a few last words.

"Father. . ." Greg whispered.

The priest now focused his attention on Greg. "Yes?"

"See you in hell," said a smiling Greg as he made his way into true darkness.

# Near the Eye of the Storm

## by Kev Nivek

The rain poured heavily in the darkened alley. Roger Strickland, a former Marine and current vagabond, was searching for shelter from the torrential onslaught.

In the distance, he spotted a faint light, presumably from the one working lamppost on the block. Underneath its dim gleam, he believed he saw a light-blue awning over back doorsteps.

This vision brought him new life as he sprang forward, splashing without caution through the many puddles on his way toward sanctuary.

Passing the light, he could see the awning. It was no mirage. With a little luck, he'd sleep dry tonight.

As he approached the awning, he felt an odd sense of awe. His throat took a peculiar tumble to the pit of his stomach as his feet slowly came to a halt. The glow from the streetlight showered the baby-blue tarp with warmth on a cold, wet night.

*But the lamp's like half a block away. . .why does the light seem to be getting brighter?*

Nearly there, he turned to look back at the lamp.

Instantly, he dropped to his knees. Soaked to the bone, he looked up in terror.

"What the hell?"

The light had followed him, all right, but it didn't belong to the streetlight.

A thick, metal tentacle was attached to the now-blinding light. It fixed itself on Roger, freezing him in intense shock. Freezing wet and paralyzed on his weakened knees, Roger felt a sudden warmth as his body then elevated from the puddle he had been in.

"But—but. . ."

Roger tried to struggle but found he couldn't move a muscle. A sudden peace swept through him; his body drew closer to the light. Utter euphoria filled his soul as the beam absorbed the last of him.

*CRACK*

The tentacle zipped through the city skyline, zigzagging its way along the retractor back to the mothership.

# Welcome Home

## by Shawn Baker

It had been three months since Chet had moved in with his roommates. Overall, they had a pretty good relationship. Chet had known Rory since 6th grade. The two were inseparable. They stood side by side at graduation and kept in touch throughout adulthood. Chet had been living with his longtime girlfriend, but time had taken a toll on the young couple. They mutually decided it was best to take a break. After the split, Rory welcomed Chet into his home with open arms. Rory had a three bedroom apartment with his expectant girlfriend, Vanessa. It wasn't hard for the couple to agree upon letting Chet move in. Vanessa was five months into her pregnancy at that point, and they all liked the idea of saving some money.

Chet was in a particularly good mood today. His roomies were getting ready to leave town for the weekend. Vanessa was having her baby shower in Vermont, where the majority of her family lived. He loved his roommates, but the past couple of weeks had been tough. There was a palpable tension throughout the house, especially between Chet and Vanessa. Vanessa hated that Chet smoked in the house, and Chet hated her cats. They were both on edge and due for some much needed time apart.

Chet was packing a bowl when he heard a knock on his bedroom door. "Who is it?"

"Rory, bro."

"Come in, ya douche." Rory opened the door and entered with a smirk on his face.

"Nice. You about to spark that up?"

"Nah. I was gonna wait until you guys rolled out. Why...you wanna hit it?"

"Please. It's a long drive to Vermont. It's even longer when you have a pregnant woman who's about to pop, riding shotgun." They both laughed.

"Yeah, I bet."

Chet lit up the bowl and passed it to Rory. Rory took a big hit and proceeded to cough to the point of tears. "Damn, bro! Don't die, Rory."

"Fuck you, man." Chet continued to smoke while his friend gained his breath.

"I better get on the road," said Rory. "Vanessa's downstairs waiting on me. I just wanted to say peace out to my boy. I know you're gonna enjoy having the place to yourself all weekend."

"You bet your sweet ass I am. I'm gonna walk around this bitch butt-booty naked the whole time!"

"I know that's right. That's what I'd be doing." They both chuckled.

Rory stood up. The two exchanged fist bumps, then Rory left the room. Chet waited until he heard the front door open, close, and lock before making his way downstairs.

Chet entered the kitchen to find the leftover spaghetti he had thawing in the sink, scattered all over the floor.

"DAMN THESE CATS! I HATE YOU MOTHERFUCKERS! WHERE THE FUCK ARE YOU!?!?!" Chet angrily stomped through the apartment, searching for the feline culprits. One had hid behind the washer and dryer, thus making him unreachable. The other one was hiding behind the couch. Chet whacked her twice with the broom. She ran out from behind the couch and darted upstairs to Rory and Vanessa's room.

"YOU STAY YOUR ASS UP THERE! I DON'T WANNA SEE YOUR STUPID, FURRY ASS-FACE AGAIN! FUCKING BITCH!"

Chet smoked another bowl to calm himself down. He had had it with these cats. This kind of thing had become an everyday occurrence. Chet felt so disrespected by Vanessa. He tried to level with her and work together to come to a solution, but she wasn't having it. Enough was enough.

Sunday came and Chet's roommates were on their way home from Vermont. He felt it necessary to greet their return properly. He'd decided to make them dinner. Chet hoped it would help relieve a bit of the tension that had been between him and Vanessa. Chet received a text from Rory, letting him know they were about an hour out. Chet made sure to let Rory know for them to come home hungry. Chet started gathering the ingredients and got to work.

Rory and Vanessa arrived to the aroma of a homecooked meal.

"Oh my, that smells good," claimed Vanessa.

"It does," replied Rory.

Exhausted from the drive, they dropped their bags and nested on the couch.

"Hello, roomies," said Chet as he brought them each a plate.

"Wow, Chet. You didn't have to do this for us," said Vanessa.

"It was my pleasure. I know things haven't been great around here lately, so I thought I'd do something to brighten the mood."

"Well, thank you, Chet. I appreciate it."

"Me too. Are you not going to eat?" wondered Rory.

"I already had a plate. I couldn't wait. It looked too damn good."

Rory and Vanessa wasted no time digging into the food. Then ten minutes had gone by before either of them had said a word.

"Where are the cats?" asked Vanessa.

"I think they're upstairs. I haven't seen them in a while."

There was a brief, yet awkward silence.

"Great spaghetti, huh?" Chet asked with a grin as he took a sip of his wine.

# Coming to Terms
## by Kev Nivek

Frank's fingers frantically fumbled the front padlock. After accepting the combination, the door slid open, revealing the chaos that was his living room. Stepping in, Frank dove for the couch, dodging the orange blur headed for his face. Looking to his right, he locked eyes with the culprit: his giggling six-year-old son Mason.

"What'd I tell you about playing Hoverball in the house?" Frank's tone was stern, but his smile gave him away. With a devilish grin, his youngest took off down the hallway.

"You're doing such a great job babysitting," Frank called down the hall to his oldest boys Billy and Jason as he then entered the kitchen.

Tossing his keycard and phone on the kitchen table, Frank called out to his only daughter. "Jenny! You here? Who's watching Mason?!"

"She's not home yet," someone replied from the hall. He couldn't quite tell if it was Jason or Billy's voice.

Well, where is she?" Frank barked, waiting impatiently for a response.

"I dunno!" the same voice answered after a slight pause.

Panic swelled inside Frank as he began to pace the room desperately, thinking of the places she could be. He didn't remember hearing anything about any practice or a project after school today. He sped to the kitchen table and fumbled with his phone. The recent news reports of terrorist-fronted kidnappings were running through his mind as he typed her UEID chip number into his app. Sweat dripped from his forehead, soon blurring the screen. Furiously scrubbing his sleeve before working on his brow, the blinking blue dot finally appeared at a precise location: the high school library. Sighing in relief, Frank turned to the hallway with instructions for dinner.

*"Ooof!"* Spit flung from Frank as a blow to the gut knocked the wind right out of him. Falling back, he caught himself on the kitchen counter. Struggling to catch his breath, he braced himself.

"Sorry, Dad," Jason muttered, rubbing his head.

"It's all right, Jay. . .just be careful. And turn that news broadcast off. I don't want your brother having those invasion nightmares again."

Frank turned to yell for Bill but found his eldest now sitting at the kitchen counter. Eyes merely inches from the 3D gaming screen projecting from it, his right hand worked the controls on the monitor.

"Dad, will you sign for this game? It's free," Billy informed Frank without looking up from the counter.

"Maybe, but what is it?" Frank didn't want some Vamp or Ghoul popping up to scare his other children.

"It's called Earth Defense; it's a tower defense game. Aliens are attacking Earth in their spaceships and you build up the Earth's defense. Starting with your own neighborhood, that is. It's really cool, Dad. You've gotta do it!"

Frank held up his right hand to settle Billy down. "What's the age requirement?"

"It's 10 and up. You can set the password. We won't let Mason play." Frank reached for the Interhome Holotablet controller on the coffee table.

"Go ahead, I guess. Send me the link," he grumbled at Billy.

He was behind on dinner without Jenny home to help start it. The boys never wanted to help but were quick to ask for a status update. Billy moved his right hand on the 3D controls and flicked his wrist toward his father. A second later, the app popped up on Frank's Holotab.

Placing his thumb on the home screen scanner, Frank skipped the manual sign up for the app. Soon a new page popped up, reading *Terms and Conditions* and followed by an endless sea of legal jargon.

Frustrated, Frank skimmed down to the bottom as quickly as his wrist could flick, eventually reaching the bottom of the agreement. He quickly clicked on the box reading the following: *I accept the UEE Terms, Conditions, and Privacy Policy.*

A voice projected through the Holotab, "Please look at the camera and say your full name—after the beep— to verify your download."

"Frank William Odom." Awkwardly, he stared at the tablet in his hands until it beeped in confirmation. He sat the Holotab back down on the table and returned to the kitchen. "Time to make dinner."

***

A pounding at the door awoke Frank in a panic the next morning. He hopped out of bed, tripping over his slippers as he slid into his thick robe. The knocking became louder and more frequent as he approached the door. Frank, about as impatient as his visitors now, fought with the lock before angrily swinging the door open.

"Morning, sir!" a young UEDU officer greeted with a Holotab in hand. Frank glanced back at the soldiers behind him before the officer held the tablet up to his face. The tablet's speaker boomed, *"Frank William Odom."*

"That you, sir?" The officer's stare made Frank feel uneasy.

"Yes. . .I'm Frank Odom. What—uh, what is this all about?" Frank stammered.

The young officer did not look up from his Holotab as he pressed on. "Earth Defense download Conditions: Section 24.8 states that in the event of an actual UCT invasion, I hereby relinquish ownership of my home to the UEDU for acquisition and upgrade in order to assist with defense tactics until the threat of attack has been officially rescinded by the UE Council."

Frank tried to protest but was pushed back by the small wave of troops that then rushed into his home. He begged the officer to reconsider, but the man didn't seem to hear him over the roar of the trench digger.

# A FAMILIAR STRANGER
## BY SHAWN BAKER

Being the new kid on the block is never fun, unless you're one of the Wahlbergs. I, however, am not. I am Brandon Silvers—just a fourteen-year-old kid from New Knavish, Ohio. My mom passed away this summer from breast cancer, so I'm now living with my grandparents in Collinsville, Kentucky. Not a bad little town if you're into muddin' and fishin'. I am interested in neither of those things.

One thing I do love though is basketball. I love everything about it. I love playing it. I love watching it. Hell, I even dream about it quite a bit. I was guaranteed a spot on the JV team back home, but these days? I'll be lucky to make the freshmen team up here. Say what you want about Kentuckians, but these people LIVE AND BREATHE basketball. Ever wonder why Kentucky doesn't have an NBA team? That's because they have the UK Wildcats. Down in the Bluegrass state, UK basketball is larger than life. They also have the Louisville Cardinals, if you're into that kind of thing.

So with that said, all these kids are bred to hunt, fish, and shoot basketball. I definitely have my work cut out for me if I want to secure a spot on this team. According to my grandpa and local media, the Collinsville Colonels have a pretty prestigious program. They're ranked second in the state, behind the Mayhew Navajos. Tryouts are a week away and I've been practicing every night for as long as I can. My grandma usually has to call me in. I am my hardest critic. I put myself through hell when it comes to training. I am determined to make this team, no matter what.

Tryout day is here and I couldn't be more nervous. Not that I am worried about how I will perform, but more about how I will be perceived by my teammates. School has been in session for about two months now, and I have yet to make a "friend." I am naturally pretty quiet in most aspects of life, but I come out of my shell once I hit the hardwood. I was considered a leader on my teams in Ohio, but I'd been playing with the same group of guys since grade school. I developed into that role over time. I earned the respect of those guys through hard work and effort on the court. These Collinsville guys don't know me from Adam. We shall see how this goes. . .

Including myself, there were about fifty kids who showed up. The coach split us up into groups of ten and had us run five-on-five, full court. First team to twenty one wins. My group was the third to play. I was confident in my team. I hadn't seen any of these kids play before, but we had a height advantage. This kid named Bo was in my grade and stood six-foot-nine. He'd be playing center for us. We had a set of twins,

Greg and Timmy Cole. Greg played the four spot and Timmy played point guard. I played shooting guard. The kid playing the three spot for us was named Alan Monroe. Funny thing about Alan is he looked so damn familiar. The whole time we were waiting to play, I'd find myself looking at him as much as I could without being noticeable. I knew we had a couple of classes together, but the familiarity ran far beyond that. I felt like I knew this kid from somewhere else. But I just couldn't quite put my finger on exactly where.

Coach blew his whistle and called our group up. With our teams already decided, we were ready to ball. We won the jump and were on our way down the court. Timmy played point and brought the ball down court for us. For a short white kid, this guy had ball-control abilities out of this world. He crossed over the opposing PG and lobbed up an alley oop to Bo for the dunk. Things were off to a great start and then stayed that way. Alan and I hooked up for a few assists between the two of us. I scored twelve of our twenty-three points. I shot two-for-two from three-point land, with one of those being the game-winning shot.

And Coach seemed impressed with us. As a team, we were thrilled with each other. We played a great game together. Tryouts came to a close, with Coach informing us that the rosters would be posted in our locker room by the end of the week.

I was waiting outside for my grandpa to pick me up when Alan approached me.

"Hey, man, good shit out there today! You seem to have a great feel for the game," said Alan.

"Thanks, dude. Same goes for you. Your post game is pretty impressive."

He smiled from the compliment. "Thanks, bro. I appreciate that."

We stood in silence briefly, nodding at each other out of respect.

"Hey. . .so the guys and I were going to Shaker's tonight to grab some food. Would you be down to join?" he asked.

Shaker's was the local hangout spot for teenagers. It was a diner that served the best milkshakes and burgers around. The owner was also a huge supporter of Collinsville basketball.

"Sure; sounds good," I responded.

"Cool. So we'll pick you up around six or so?"

"That works."

We exchanged cell numbers. I texted him my address and we parted ways when my grandpa arrived. I was ecstatic. Things were finally starting to look up. Alan seemed real cool. I was looking forward to bonding with the guys that night—especially since there was a chance we'd be teammates soon.

Bo and Alan picked me up at 6:15 that evening. We went to Shaker's as planned. The Cole twins met us there. Timmy also brought his girlfriend, so we made fun of him every chance we got. We landed a table by the window. I was the only one who needed to look at a menu. Bo took it upon himself to be the Shaker's spokesperson, making recommendations left and right.

"So, Brandon. . .what brings you to Baltimore?" asked Greg.

"My mom passed away back in June from breast cancer."

There was a sympathetic silence.

"Damn, man, that sucks!" said Alan, who was sitting to my right.

"Yeah, I miss her. My grandparents are pretty cool, though. They've been super helpful through all this."

"That's what's up, man," said Bo.

"Do you get to see your Dad at all?" asked Timmy.

"No. He passed away when I was eight."

There was another sympathetic silence.

"My dad passed away when I was eight as well, man," said Alan.

"Really?" I replied.

"Yeah; but I never knew him. My mom doesn't talk about him much. I do have a picture of him holding me the day I was born, though that is it."

"Mine was barely around either. He drove a truck, so we rarely saw him," I said.

The conversation was put on hold as the waitress delivered our food. I settled on the BBQ Bacon Burger with a chocolate shake. Alan had the same, except he opted for the strawberry shake instead. The food definitely lived up to hype around town. We ate our food and left shortly after 9 p.m.

The following Wednesday came with a buzz surrounding it. Coach had announced on Tuesday that the rosters would be posted before the end of school Wednesday. He followed through on his promise. Alan and I decided to go look together at the end of the day. We arrived to a small crowd of guys eyeing the results. Some were happy, some were not. Once Alan and I made it to the front of the pack, we were pleased to see we both made the JV team. Not only did we make the lineup, but we were also listed as starters. Not bad for a couple of Freshmen.

"Dude! Know what this means?" Alan asked.

"What's that?"

"If we play well this year, our chance of making Varsity sophomore year is hella strong."

"Hell yeah, man!"

"We need to start practicing ASAP. What are you doing tonight?" inquired Alan.

"Well, I don't have any homework, so I was just gonna go home and practice on my game."

"Perfect! You should come to my house. You could join us for dinner."

"Yeah, that should be fine. I just have to run it by my grandparents first."

"Sweet. Just text me and let me know what they say. If they say yes, I can talk my sister into  picking you up. She thinks you're cute. . .so it shouldn't be hard to convince her."

"Make sure she knows I think the same!"

We both chuckled.

My grandmother was initially hesitant about letting me loose on a school night, but they ultimately decided it was fine. I texted Alan the news. He and his sister Clarissa were at my house in no time. We arrived at Alan's shortly before 4 p.m. His mom hadn't gotten home from work yet. We went upstairs to change and get ready to hoop. Alan went to the bathroom first. I chilled in his room. He had some of the coolest posters I'd ever seen. Sports icons such as Larry Bird, John Wall, DeMarcus Cousins, and Anthony Davis were plastered all over. Lots of UK Wildcats. As I was walking around his room, I noticed a picture on his dresser. It was of a man holding a baby, which I assumed to be a little Alan. I'd seen the man in the picture before. In fact, I felt like I'd seen the same picture before.

Alan walked into the room. "Bathroom's all yours, brother."

"Hey, Alan, are you the baby in this picture?"

"Yeah. That's the picture I was telling you about with my dad. It's the only one I have."

Chills rose up my back, causing the hairs on my neck to stand up as I weighed the possibilities in my mind.

"Alan. . .what was your father's name?"

"James. . .why?"

I stood frozen in place. I felt like my eyes were playing tricks on me. How could it be that Alan's dad looked EXACTLY like my dad and even had the same name?

"Your dad's last name was Monroe, right?" I asked.

"No, I took my mom's last name. My dad's last name was. . .Silvers."

We looked at each other in complete bewilderment.

"Alan. . .my dad's name was James Issac Silvers."

"So was mine."

We stood side by side, staring at the picture on his dresser. It all made sense now. No wonder he looked so familiar. I had been trying to figure it out since the day I met him. Now we knew the answer. He is a spitting image of our father.

# LOST AND FOUND
## BY KEV NIVEK

Street lights flickered on as the car sped down the alley. The sunset's purple backdrop faded to black—fast—as stars emerged in the new night sky. A full moon hung high above the trees as he whipped into the driveway. He had almost beat the darkness home.

Tripping as he tore through the yard, he fumbled for his keys once stumbling up the front steps. Fighting with the deadbolt, he began cursing under his breath.

"Stupid mother. . ." With a creak, the door opened. Quickly, he slid inside, wincing while the bolt clanged into place. Moving as silently as possible, he made his way to the stairs. The living room's wood floor betrayed him, announcing his every step.

Reaching the hallway, he froze. At the bottom of the steps, the bathroom door hung open. The tips of his ears burned red as the voices in his head argued over whether it had been left that way.

With a prolonged breath, he rubbed his thumb and index finger together for a moment, in an effort to quiet his anxiety. It hardly helped. Sweat began to roll down his temple as he poked his head into the bathroom.

A shallow wave of calm washed over him as he finally appreciated the somewhat transparent shower curtain he'd so foolishly bought online.

All clear. Leaving the door open, he made a mental note as he crept back to the stairs.

The creaking living room floor was nothing compared to the painful groan of each step.

Resorting to an awkward crawl, he climbed to the loft on all fours, peaking over the railing as he hit the top step. His bedroom door was closed and the loft looked exactly as he had left it. Despite this good omen, he continued to crawl as he inched his way to the door, forever swearing off any unforgiving wood floor.

He paused for a long moment upon reaching his bedroom. Ear to the ground, he focused every ounce of his energy into laying perfectly still. A minute masqueraded as an hour while he mustered the courage to reach for the door handle.

With a quick twist, he popped the door open, sliding back in precautionary self-defense as he did so.

He held back briefly, scanning the loft for a nearby weapon. Only a sandal was handy. Slowly moving into a crouch, he headed for the door. His free hand grasped the wooden frame when he peaked in.

His room was a disaster.

It was the disaster that he was used to, however. And after seeing his closet door firmly shut, he was hit with another calming wave. He sensed some of the tension in his shoulders subside, but with a swift shake of his head, he snapped back into focus.

He dropped the sandal upon entering his room, darting for his dresser in the far corner. Diving to the ground, he reached under the dresser for the black case tucked away in its hiding spot. The haunted wood groaned again, but he paid it no attention as his fingers struck plastic gold.

Dragging the case out from the dresser, his eyes bulged with fear. He wouldn't need to open it to see that it was empty. The wood floor screamed behind him.

Jumping back, he slid to the corner, staring in bewilderment at what had emerged from his closet. The dark eyes he stared into were his own.

A clean-shaven doppelganger stood before him, smirking devilishly. In his left hand, he held a nickel-plated Beretta 92fs.

Lookin' for this?" With a grin, the duplicate pulled back the hammer.

*I almost beat the darkness home.*

# UNDER WATCH
## BY SHAWN BAKER

New Knavish Sanitarium
September, 1949

Michael sat in the chair across from Dr. Schlegel's desk, both hands pressed against his forehead. He had not slept in two days. The ringing inside his head had intensified and made it impossible to focus on anything else.

"Michael. . .on a scale of one to ten, how severe is the pain you're experiencing?"

"Ahhhh," groaned Michael as he leaned back in his chair, his hands still pressed firmly against his skull.

"Michael..."

"I DON'T KNOW, DOC! IT TIPS THE FUCKING SCALE."

"I see. . .when did the ringing start?"

"About a week ago."

"Do you happen to recall what you were doing when the ringing started?"

"I was digging."

"Digging?"

Michael removed his hands from his face, sat up straight in his chair and looked Dr. Schlegal square in the eyes.

"Yes," replied Michael.

"And why were you digging?"

"I don't remember."

The doctor looked up from his notebook with a look of disbelief written across his face.

"I honestly don't," Michael reassured.

"Okay," said the doctor as he looked down at his pad and continued writing.

"All I remember is that it was dark and raining. I kept digging until I collapsed. I must've blacked out or something because I woke up in the hole the next morning. I heard Mother screaming frantically."

The doctor looked up from his pad once more. "I see. Well, I am glad you came in, Michael. I can—"

"I don't want some bullshit ibuprofen prescription," Michael interrupted. "I want Stoginite and I want you to help me get it."

"Michael, I can't. . ."

"Don't give me that bullshit, Schlegal! I know you have a guy who can get banned pharmaceuticals. You've used him before for my father."

"Michael, it's not that simple."

Michael rose from his seat, reached in his blazer pocket and pulled out a check. He walked over to Dr. Schlegal's desk and planted it firmly down on top. The doctor's eyes widened when he saw the amount.

"Get me the fucking Stoginite, Schlegal," said Michael in a calm, yet serious tone.

The doctor sat quietly as he stared at the check, weighing his options. After careful contemplation, he looked Michael in the eyes as he reached for the check and placed it in his desk drawer.

"Good," said Michael. "Very good."

Michael sat back down in his chair across from Dr. Schlegal's desk.

"We will need to keep you here for the first five to seven days—for observation. The side effects are virtually unknown. Quite frankly, with it being manufactured in the Soviet Union, it's best that we take all the necessary precautions."

"That's fine. When can we start the trial?" asked Michael.

"I can have it here by the end of the month. Let's shoot for Monday, October 3rd. If anything changes, I'll contact you immediately."

"Thank you."

Michael rose to his feet, approaching Dr. Schlegal as he stood up as well. The two shook hands and Michael exited the office.

✳ ✳ ✳

October 3rd had arrived and couldn't have come sooner. Michael's headaches had intensified as the ringing grew louder. Michael completed the intake process and proceeded to the inpatient ward where he was met by Dr. Schlegal.

"Good to see you, Michael."

"Wish I could say the same, Doc. No offense."

"None taken. Follow me."

Dr. Schlegal led Michael to his room where they were met by a nurse. The nurse was an older woman—short and plump. She was holding a silver tray. The tray contained a small, clear cup of water and two white pills.

"Michael, this wonderful young lady is Ms. Duvall. She is the Head Nurse of this ward. She'll help make sure you receive the best care possible."

"Hello, Michael," said Ms. Duvall.

"Hi," said Michael, forcing a slight half-hearted smile.

"Well then, why don't we get started?" asked Dr. Schlegal.

"Sounds good. I'm ready," Michael responded.

Ms. Duvall handed Michael the two pills, followed by a cup of water. Michael tossed them into his mouth and leaned his head back as he chased them with water.

"Wonderful," said Dr. Schlegal. "So Michael, go ahead and make yourself comfortable. Ms. Duvall will be back to check on you here shortly."

"All right. I am just going to relax a bit. I brought plenty of reading materials."

"Good call," replied Dr. Schlegal.

The doctor and Ms. Duvall exited the room. He slipped into the gown provided by the hospital. He grabbed his copy of 1984 from his suitcase and got into bed. He was forty-nine pages in when Ms. Duvall made her return.

"How is everything, Michael?"

"Good as it can be, I guess."

"I see you're reading 1984. I just finished it recently. Great book."

"I like it so far."

"Have the headaches weakened at all since taking the Stoginite?"

"No. . .but the ringing has quieted a bit."

"Well, that's a start! I am sure that after a good night's sleep, you will be right as rain."

"I certainly hope so," replied Michael.

"Well, I will leave you be for the remainder of the evening. If you need anything before bed, don't hesitate to ask. I'll be just outside the door at my desk."

"Thank you."

"You're very welcome. Good night, dear."

"Night."

Michael watched Ms. Duvall as she left the room. He was impressed with her figure. For an older woman, she had an impeccable backside. Michael continued to read his book for a while longer before calling it a night. He placed the book on the nightstand next to his bed, turned off the lamp, and rolled over onto his right side.

Facing the window, he gazed at the stars. The ringing grew faint, but still pecked at his brain. He closed his eyes and imagined he was on a boat with his father. The two used to go fishing every summer before his father's health had declined. His father had passed earlier that year and Michael was still grieving. He lay there in bed, picturing the two comparing fish they had caught. It brought a smile to his face as he faded into a deep sleep.

***

Three days had passed since Michael had arrived for his inpatient treatment. The ringing was faint during the day but was as loud as a fire alarm in his dreams. This caused him to sleep restlessly and wake up constantly throughout the night. The headaches were as strong as ever.

On the fourth night, he convinced Ms. Duvall to give him an extra two pills with dinner. Initially hesitant, she was swayed when he slid her a hundred-dollar bill. Michael swallowed the four pills and proceeded to eat his chocolate pudding. He sat in his bed, now reading The Third Man by Graham Greene. He dozed off, with the novel in hand.

He was awoken to the ear-splitting ring hammering through his head. This caused a headache so fierce that it made him nauseous. He stumbled his way through his room to the doorway. He exited his room, holding his head with both hands as he made way to the ward restroom. He approached the sink and began splashing water onto his face. He looked up at the mirror, only to discover that his nose was bleeding and his pupils were dilated.

Michael rinsed the blood from his face and took a paper towel from the dispenser. He ripped off two pieces and stuffed one in each nostril. He threw the remainder of the paper towel into the trash receptacle. Michael walked over to the urinal and began to urinate. He slowly raised his head and looked over to his right— where his eyes were met by another man's.

This man was also dressed in a hospital gown. The two men made eye contact for ten seconds or so before the silence was broken.

"See something you like, faggot?" antagonized the man.

Michael stood frozen in place, eyes remaining fixated on the man.

"You can look away now, fucker," said the man aggressively.

Michael tucked away his penis, and turned toward the man, now standing toe to toe.

"What's your fucking problem?" asked the man.

Michael continued to ignore the man's retorts. He stared blankly at the man before grabbing him by the head and slamming it into the urinal. The man was knocked unconscious from the impact. The ringing in Michael's head had now turned into an ominous whisper.

*Kill. . .feed. . .kill. . .feed.*

Michael reached down, pulled the man's head up and began to feast on his neck. Michael's attention was redirected toward the restroom door as it swung open. Ms. Duvall stood in the doorway with a ghastly expression upon her face.

"BY GOD, MICHAEL. . .WHAT HAVE YOU DONE?" Ms. Duvall shrieked.

Michael's eyes fixated on the nurse as he rose to his feet, growling as he did so. Frozen in fear, Ms. Duvall leered helplessly at Michael. He charged the nurse and ripped her throat out of her neck with his teeth. She fell backwards onto the floor. She laid there on the cold tile, bleeding to death as she witnessed Michael release a ferocious roar.

He then proceeded to sprint down the main hall of the ward until he reached the window at the end. He flung forward, shattering the glass as he made his escape through the night.

# ON THE SPOT
## BY KEV NIVEK

The flash was blinding. He held his hand to his face in a failing effort to shade his tired, covered eyes.

"Why'd you have to do that, Johnny? You ruined the picture," Denise chastised her older brother, even as he stumbled backward against the wall.

"Look, I'm sorry. I can't fucking see." His fingers pressed against his eyes in agony.

*Please God, what is going on with me?*

Burning, his eyes were overcome with a flood of tears. No matter how he tried, he couldn't bring himself to open them for longer than a few seconds.

"John, you doin' ok?" John's best buddy Bruce bent over to check on him.

"Yeah, man; I'm fine," he mumbled through salty tears. "I just need to find the bathroom real quick."

"Closest one's over there." Bruce gestured forward as he continued. "It's straight ahead at the visitors center. Just past those two pavilions; head around the back to get to the men's room."

"Thanks, Bruce," John grunted as he left, his hands covering his hardly open eyes.

"Hey, John. . .need a hand, buddy? I can show ya the quickest way!" Bruce hollered half-heartedly after his friend.

John turned back to wave Bruce off, again grunting until he suddenly slipped in the mud.

"I'm fine. I've got it from here, Bruce!" John shouted back as he continued.

Bruce turned towards the table, catching Denise's eye as he did. They looked at each other for a brief eternity before Bruce reached for his rye glass. Denise looked away and silently sobbed into her sweater.

***

A triumphant stumble onto the pavement meant that John had passed the pavilions and progressed to the VC.

Shuffling to his left with his arms outstretched, he stopped for a quick breath once he touched the wall.

As he stood, he felt a shivering warmth spread over him. Frozen for a moment, he cautiously held up his head. Using his forearm to shield his sensitive eyes, he looked up at the source.

The light above the corner of the building cast down its warm light, outshining the Sun itself.

A puzzled Johnny pressed on. *Why would the park have such a bright light on during the day?*

Using the wall as his guide, he made his way along the side of the building.

Reaching the far corner, he shuddered again when he felt the unceasing warmth wash over him. He didn't bother to inspect the light this time.

His eyes had started leaking again so he kept his head down and his hands high on the wall. Inching his way to the door, John began to sweat profusely. He stepped from the wall, just for a moment. Long enough to use both forearm sleeves to wipe the collection off sweat, tears, and mucus from his face.

It hardly helped.

John's skin was unbearably hot as he lunged for the blurry green rectangle that he hoped to be the men's room door. The light felt closer now. He felt its heat hovering just above his head.

With all of his strength, John pushed himself towards the door. Despite his effort, he hadn't moved an inch.

The light had surrounded him. His fears fled from him as the light burned brighter.

A thick metallic bulb hovered above him. Its welcoming light lifted Johnny from his feet. He felt a rush of euphoria as it absorbed him completely.

*CRACK*

Blasting back into the atmosphere within an instant, the pod was gone.

"Yeeeaaahhhh!" Shane enthused as he walked into the kitchen. "The Facebook event is officially created, my dude."

"That's what's up," Tevin responded as he rummaged through the fridge. "Dude, we are completely out of beer."

"No way. There oughta be some Heinies left over from the other night," Shane insisted.

"No, sir. We are dry as fuck in here," replied Tevin.

"Damn. It's all good, bro. We can just pick some up at the liquor store. We need to go swoop some whiskey anyways," said Shane.

"Cool."

The two roommates hopped in Shane's '97 Toyota Camry and drove four blocks north to the state store. They arrived at a nearly empty parking lot.

"Niicceee," Shane effused as he pulled into the parking spot closest to the entrance.

"Probably helps that we came first thing in the morning," Tevin added.

"True," Shane agreed.

The two exited the vehicle and walked toward the liquor store entrance. They were greeted by a vagrant who was leaning against the trash can out front.

"Hey, can y'all spare some change? I'm tryna catch the bus," claimed the man.

"I don't carry cash, man. Sorry," said Shane.

"How 'bout you, youngblood?" asked the man, directing his question toward Tevin.

"I am tapped out," said Tevin.

"Well, can ya spot a brotha on a tall boy or sumthin?" asked the man, redirecting his question to Shane.

Shane ignored the man as he and Tevin entered the liquor store.

"I see how it is! Stingy muthafuckas," exclaimed the man.

The two roommates were relieved to be in the store. They walked down the first aisle and made a right at the end. They examined the shelves before agreeing on a bottle of Crown Royal.

"I think I am gonna grab a bottle of Jack too," said Tevin.

"That's what's up," Shane responded.

Tevin grabbed the Jack Daniels and the two headed up front. They stopped at the cooler to grab beer as well. Tevin grabbed a twelve pack of Rolling Rock and Shane grabbed a case of Budweiser.

"This should be plenty, right?" asked Shane.

"Hell yeah," Tevin agreed.

"We got mixers at the house," asked Shane.

"Yeah, we got like six two liters of Coke."

"Cool."

The two took their beverages to the counter to check out. The two split the cost in half and left. As they walked out of the store, they were stopped yet again by the same vagrant.

"Hey, can y'all break off one of them brews?" asked the man.

"Man, no!" Shane shouted.

"You ain't gotta be like that! You ain't ever heard of sharing?"

"You ain't ever heard of getting a job?" Shane fired back.

"Man, fuck you!" screamed the vagrant.

"Right back at ya, bum!" yelled Shane.

"Bro, let's go," Tevin said to his friend.

The two placed their alcohol in the back seat as the vagrant continued to yell obscenities at them. They entered the vehicle and pulled out of the parking spot. The bum kept yelling and flipped them off as they drove away.

"Man, that's why I hate going to that fucking place. It's like Bum Haven over there," said Shane as he gripped the steering wheel tightly.

"I know. Thank God we're moving soon. I hate living over here in general," Tevin replied.

"You and me both, bro."

The two pulled into their driveway and carried the goods inside. They threw the whiskey in the freezer and grabbed a beer apiece before putting them in the fridge.

"Anybody say they were coming on the event page yet?" asked Tevin.

"I don't know. I'm about to check," replied Shane as he took a swig of his Budweiser. He scrolled down the page on his phone.

"So far. . .we have three maybes, six can't-make-its, and zero coming," Shane said.

"What the fuck. . ." Tevin responded.

"I know, bro. Hopefully this doesn't turn into a snoozefest."

"No kidding. Well, I'm about to hit the shower. I will return shortly," Tevin stated.

"Sounds good. I am gonna get some tunes going in the living room. I'll have a bowl ready when ya come back down."

"Titties," Tevin effused.

✱✱✱

Tevin walked down the stairs into the living room. He was amused to find Shane slow-dancing with himself, humming to the melody with his eyes closed.

"The fuck is this?" asked Tevin.

Shane stopped dancing abruptly and turned toward his friend. The embarrassment was obvious as Shane's face turned red.

"Don't judge me, bro," Shane muttered.

"Too late," Tevin responded.

Tevin walked over to the stereo that sat on the ledge above the fireplace. He picked up the phone that was connected to the auxiliary cord and began searching for a new playlist.

"We are definitely not smoking to no slow jams, bro," Tevin said.

"You're such a hater. I'm trying to set the mood. Forgive me for wanting to get laid tonight," said Shane.

"You had your time to do that. Now it's time to get into party mode. Feel me?"

"I guess. Hater."

They both chuckled. Tevin settled on a 2000's Party Time playlist and made his way over to the sofa. The two roommates sat down, each equipped with a cold brew in hand. Shane lit the bowl, inhaled, and passed it to Tevin on his right. Tevin inhaled and passed it back to Shane.

"So what's the four-one-one on the party page? Any hits?" Tevin asked.

"I just looked a minute ago. Still nothing."

"Damn. This may be a fail after all."

"Josie texted me. She plans on stopping by after she gets off work. She's supposed to be bringing a couple of her homegirls with her."

"Oh yeah? That sounds promising," Tevin replied.

"Oh yeah. You know Josie runs with all the freaks."

"For sure. I like the sound of that."

The two continued to pass the bowl back and forth until it was cashed. Tevin sat the bowl down on the coffee table and leaned back into the sofa. A loud knock on the back door echoed through the house. The two roommates looked at each other.

"First guest," Tevin asked.

"Guess so. I'll get it," said Shane.

Shane stood up and walked through the kitchen to the back door. He opened the door, stunned by the sight of a familiar, yet unwelcomed face.

"Surprise, bitch!" exclaimed the vagrant from earlier.

The vagrant stood at the door with a pistol in hand, pointing at Shane. Frozen in fear, Shane stared at the man, unable to speak.

"Well, don't just stand there, bitch. . .let me in," said the vagrant.

Shane took a few steps back and moved to the side, allowing the vagrant to enter. The man walked inside, his gun still steadily pointed at Shane. Shane then closed the door. The vagrant looked around the kitchen, scanning the perimeter with laser focus.

"Ahhh, jackpot," stated the vagrant. He had spotted the liquor bottles that lined the countertop near the stove.

"Go ahead and grab a couple of trash bags, youngblood. Imma need you to put both those bottles of whiskey in one and all your beer in the other. Make it snappy too, fatty. I ain't got all night."

Shane moved slowly toward the cabinet under the sink and retrieved two black trash bags. He began filling the first bag, dropping in the Crown Royal first. As he reached for the Jack Daniels, Tevin entered the kitchen, armed with a silver Louisville Slugger. The vagrant began laughing hysterically.

"Are you serious, bitch? You gonna bring a bat to a gunfight? Wow!" said the vagrant.

The vagrant followed his statement with more laughter. Shane looked at Tevin hopelessly. Tevin looked back with uncertainty. The vagrant kept the gun pointed at Shane as the man opened the fridge and grabbed a beer. The vagrant opened the beer can and took a long drink, nearly finishing the whole can in one pull. He aahed with delight, smiling as he used his left thumb to scratch his brow.

Shane finished loading the first bag up with liquor. Tevin stood frozen as he watched his friend move cautiously toward the fridge, emptying it of all the beer.

"That's right. I want every last one of those," said the vagrant.

Shane filled the bag, closed the refrigerator door, and attempted to hand both bags to the vagrant.

"Not so fast," said the vagrant. "I ain't done with y'all."

The man waved his snub nose downward, signaling Shane to sit the bags down. Shane released the bags, letting them fall to the floor. The vagrant kept his gun pointed at Shane as he redirected his attention to Tevin, who stood stagnant in the doorway.

"Toss the bat on the floor towards me," demanded the vagrant.

Hesitant to do so, Tevin remained still. Tears rolled down Shane's face as he looked down at the floor.

"Did I stutta, bitch? Toss the bat over here or I'll blow your friend's fat fucking brains right out of his skull."

Shane lifted his head upward, looking Tevin in the eyes.

"Just do it, bro," Shane said softly. "Do it."

Tevin eyes filled with tears as he tossed the bat away, sighing as it landed near the vagrant.

"That's what I thought. Now y'all walk slowly into the other room," the vagrant demanded. "And don't try to be slick!"

The two roommates led the vagrant into the living room. They stopped in the middle of the room and faced the man, anticipating what was going to happen next.

"Please don't kill us," Shane squeaked, tears dropping like a waterfall.

"I'm not gonna kill you bitches," said the vagrant. "I just want all your goodies. I got the brew, now I need the weed. Yeah, I smelled that shit. Hand it over. All of it. C'mon now."

The vagrant stood firmly, holding out one hand for the weed, while aiming the gun at Tevin with the other. Tevin sighed as he turned around to grab the marijauna off the coffee table. He handed the vagrant a bag that contained a little less than a half ounce.

"I want them blunts y'all got rolled up, too," stated the vagrant. "Don't be stingy now."

"Oh, we're being stingy," asked Tevin.

"Don't get smart, bitch," responded the vagrant.

Shane grabbed the blunts off the table and handed them to the vagrant.

"I need a lighter as well," said the vagrant.

"Are you fucking kidding me?" muttered Shane under his breath.

The vagrant looked at Tevin with a serious look on his face.

"Don't make me tell ya to watch ya mouth again, youngblood."

Tevin stared at the man, biting his tongue. Shane handed the vagrant a silver BIC lighter. The vagrant placed one of the three blunts in his mouth and lit it. The roommates stood in silence as they watched the vagrant take a long puff of their blunt. Tevin's blood was boiling, his eyes piercing through the bum. The vagrant inhaled for eight seconds before releasing a cloud of smoke into the air. He coughed harshly, causing the roommates to take a couple steps back to avoid the droplets of spit being spewed. The vagrant caught his breath, followed by a long whew.

"Man, that's some good shit," said the vagrant as he examined the blunt with admiration.

"Glad you like it," said Shane.

"Don't you get cute now, pussy boy!" said the vagrant. "Y'all sit ya asses down."

The roommates did as requested, and plopped down onto the sofa. The vagrant took another long drag from the blunt, inhaling briefly this time before exhaling.

"Party on, bitches. I had a blast," said the vagrant, laughing as he turned toward the kitchen and made his way to the back door. The roommates sat still until they heard the back door slam shut.

"WHAT THE FUCK WAS THAT??" screamed Tevin.

Shane sighed in relief, throwing his head back against the sofa, grateful just to be alive.

"HE BETTER HOPE I NEVER SEE HIS ASS AGAIN. I WILL KILL THAT MOTHERFUCKER," yelled Tevin.

There was a knock at the back door. The roommates remained in place. The first knock was followed by a second, then a third.

"You really think he came back?" Shane asked quietly.

"He fucking better not have," replied Tevin with confidence, as he reached for his bat once more. Tevin stormed toward the kitchen as he heard the back door open.

"Hello?" said a female. "Anybody home?"

Tevin stopped in his tracks as three women appeared in the kitchen doorway.

"Josie!" yelled Shane with excitement, as he jumped to his feet. He quickly walked toward the ladies, brushing past Tevin as he embraced Josie with a hug.

"Damn. . .am I glad to see you," Shane said softly as he held her tightly. The two smiled as they let go of each other.

"Hey ladies," said Shane, greeting Josie's friends.

"Heyyy," said the two women in unison.

Josie observed a standing-still Tevin, his hand firmly gripping his bat.

"What's with the bat, Tevin?" Josie asked.

Tevin took a deep breath before tossing it to the side.

"It's nothing," Tevin responded. "Please tell me y'all brought some alcohol."

# SUNDOWN
## BY KEV NIVEK

It was all for love. That's what had gotten him here. That and his stupidity. As the tears welled up, he shoved the letter into the envelope, sealing it with the family crest.

The wind howled, slamming the wooden shutters against the homely cabin. Rain poured on the rooftop, punctuated by enormous thunderclaps. Lightning tore through the sky as the front door was kicked open. Jebidiah's younger brother, Zachariah strode into the room, tossing his satchel by the fireplace. The youngest Godfrey boy Jeremiah, limped in after Zach, struggling under the weight of the overloaded saddlebags he had been tasked to carry.

Falling to the ground, Jeremiah somehow managed to shut the door behind him. Jeb looked up from his desk but didn't address his brothers. Instead, he set his letter on the table and slowly put his leather gloves on.

Zach and Jerry stood staring at their shared idol, waiting and watching his every move. Gloves on, Jeb calmly walked around to the front of the table, sitting on its edge to address his family.

"Well, boys, this is it. I love you both, so I'm giving ya one last chance to turn and go. I'm not gonna hold it against you if you do. Lord knows you've both helped me more than a brother oughta have to. Now, I can't walk away from this, but you can." Jeb motioned to the soggy saddlebags. To his surprise, it was Jerry who spoke first.

"Cut the shit, Jeb. We've seen you this far. . .what's gonna stop us now?" Jerry quickly turned to Zach.

"And if this bastard backs down, he's carrying his own damn bags back to the stable!" The brothers shared a tense laugh that each one of them truly needed. As it died down to an awkward silence, Zach confirmed what Jeb already knew. Tonight, the three of them would be riding to hell together.

***

As dusk drew near, the brothers prepared for their midnight raid. Zach had just finished replacing all of Jerry's bandages. Finishing his whiskey to keep the pain at bay, Jerry was now resting his eyes to preserve energy.

Jeb knew the night would be a long one. He took a few swigs from his flask and kept the pipe full of tobacco. He'd cleaned his pistols three times each. *Maybe I should clean the rifles. . .there should be enough time.*

Jeb shot up in his chair, kicking it away from him as he stood. He went straight for the saddlebags on the ground, frantically searching for the hunting rifles and

Jerry's shotgun. He muttered to himself in frustration as his search found nothing. Zach noticed his brother's antics.

"You okay there, Jeb?" He received a threatening glare that seemed to plant Jeb's voice in his ear.

*Where the fuck are the guns?*

Coming to briefly, Jerry answered the question in a dream-like daze. "Shit, boys, I left your rifles in the stable," he mumbled as he crept back into dreamland.

Jeb was furious, but now wasn't the time to show it. It was his fault his brothers were even there, and there was nowhere else to place the blame. He held his tongue and stood up, dusting himself off and grabbing his pistols from the desk before placing them in his holsters.

"Zach, can you cover the window? I'm gonna check on the horses once I have the guns. They have a long night ahead of 'em." Zach sprung to his feet, grabbing the hammer by his chair. Quickly yanking two nails from the top board covering the window, he gave himself just enough room to see the barn from where he stood.

"Jerry, we're gonna have to head out in a bit. So grab yourself a cup of coffee," Jeb ordered as he threw the front door open with aid from the roaring wind. "And shut this damn thing behind me, will ya?"

Jerry was halfway to the coffee pot in the cabin's back corner, so the hammer-holding Zach left his post and smacked the door with a few planks nailed into them.

"That oughta hold!" Zach said triumphantly.

*∗∗∗

Jerry had to sit down to pour the coffee. His hands weren't trembling anymore. Steam rose from the ceramic mug as the brown-gold filled it. Jerry took a deep breath before bringing the cup to his lips.

A gigantic crack was heard as something crashed into the back of the tiny cabin. The scalding coffee spilled all over Jerry as he did his best to dive back to the front entrance near Zach.

Zach raced to his kid brother and helped him up, handing Jerry his twin six-shooters after propping him down in a chair facing the back entrance. Zach moved to the other side of the door. He pulled his pistols out as the crashing got louder and more frequent.

"Jeb! We could use a little help here!" Zach screamed as he aimed at the back door.

"Wait till it breaks through, Jerry. Don't waste a bullet," Zach urged, adjusting the grip on his pistols.

The crashes intensified; the brothers heard the creaking of broken wood as the whole wall seemed ready to collapse. The repeating blasts sent splinters raining from the ceiling.

"Jeb!" Jerry cried out for his brother as the door was smashed again, barely hanging from the frame. The planks the boys had used to keep the wind out were now their last line of defense against the indescribable, incoming onslaught.

***

"Come on, dammit," Zach whispered to himself as he reached out to Jeb with his mind, hoping to somehow draw him back to the cabin.

*BOOSH*

The door exploded into pieces. Splinters and shards rushed at the brothers like arrows. With their eyes shielded, the boys began to blast away.

They could hardly see the shrouded figure as it crept down to enter the six-foot doorway. A lucky slug caught it in the chest but did nothing to slow it down. Barreling forward, only the whites of its eyes could be seen. Larger and wider than that of a human, this creature's cold gaze shook Zach to his core. He closed his eyes and fired with both pistols, aiming blindly at those miserable, haunting eyes. The beast took two more shots in the shoulder, finally knocking it back a step.

Hissing in anger, the beast leaped to the ceiling. Massive, clawed feet held the support beams, allowing it to hang like a bat. The next few blasts from the Godreys guns came nowhere near it, and the boys were running out of rounds.

***

Jerry noticed the beast's new perch first. Unable to believe his eyes, he wondered if he had one too many from the bottle.

"Roof! It's up in the rafters, Jerry!" Zach's words confirmed what Jerry still could not believe. Biting his lip, he leaned back in pain, using the back of the chair to steady his aim. With a breath, he pulled back on the trigger.

This shot caught the creature in its other shoulder. It writhed in pain and shrieked as it reared back, readying to lunge. It cocked back its arm and hit Jerry with the back of its ghoulish hand. Jerry went flying into the brick chimney like a rag doll, crashing with a sickening thud.

"Jerry!" Zach looked around in shock, barely able to dodge a swing from the creature that was aimed at him. Diving to the ground near his limply laying brother, he turned to fire on the ghoul, but his hammer clicked in defiance. The gun was empty. The creature again shrieked angrily, ready to destroy Zach. The look in its eyes held fury. It was going to enjoy this. Rearing back, it inhaled deeply, preparing to attack.

*BLAMM*

A rifle blast from the front window took the beast's head clean off. The creep's body fell from the ceiling and landed with a crash, laying still—save for some twitching fingers. Zach then scrambled to his feet. Completely bewildered, he was broken from his spell by a shout from outside.

"Zach! Jer! You gonna let me in or what?"

***

Jerry's entire body throbbed in pain. He tried to open his swollen eyes. When he finally managed to, he was horrified. The lifeless body of the creature was lumped onto the floor, its headless body was just too close for comfort. Wheezing through his broken nose, Jerry attempted to lift himself onto the nearest chair but a sharp pain in his ribs kept him from doing so.

Leaning up against the fireplace, Jerry could hear his brothers gearing up the horses outside the wide-open front door. The wood swayed constantly in the cool wind. Jerry's eyes grew heavy as he began to doze off again.

"Jeremiah. . ." a sickly voice whispered in Jerry's ear. Certain it was in his mind, he ignored it and kept his eyes closed. His brothers would be ready soon, and he needed to rest while he had the chance.

"Jeremiah. Join us."

This time, the voice felt closer. He fell off the fireplace, sliding to his right into the corner of the room. Jerry stared at the creature with intent. He was certain that this sonofabitch was only talking to him. Feeling around for his flask, his hands found his trusty shotgun instead. Smiling from familiarity and newfound confidence, Jerry whipped the stock to his shoulder and aimed at the carcass.

"You were saying?" Jerry licked his lips in anticipation, ready to blast this heathen to kingdom come. His trigger finger twitched as he nervously adjusted his grip. Sweat came quickly, causing the adjustments to increase in pace. There was a stinging pain in his face as sweat met with the drying blood around his eyes. Subconsciously, Jerry rocked back and forth on the floor.

"Come on, you bastard!" he muttered to himself. *Give me half a reason.* His heart pounded in his chest. An intense wave of energy fueled Jerry as he felt the blood coursing through his veins. That thing broke him in half. He was itching to return the favor.

"We can fix you, child." There was the voice again in Jerry's left ear. He spun and fired, blasting blindly from the hip. The slug struck the chimney, scattering chunks of brick in all directions. The kick from the shotgun hit him like a mule. Writhing in pain, he curled up on the floorboards. Above him, he heard Jeb and Zach running in. They called for him, but their voices seemed so far away. As he faded, that damned voice rang out in his ear again. . .

"We'll see you soon, Jeremiah."

# CRIPPLED INSIDE
## BY SHAWN BAKER

My eyes open to utter darkness. I find myself in my den, sitting in my leather recliner. I must've fallen asleep again. I hate when that happens—because I know my wife will bitch about it later. I can hear Angie now. *You spend more time in that damn den than you spend with me or Kyra!*

I attempt to rise to my feet, but fail tremendously. I'm unable to move whatsoever. I try to move in a forward motion and also side to side. No luck either way. It feels like someone covered my back with Gorilla Glue and stuck me in this chair. I double-check my arms that lie along the arm rests. They look resistant free. No straps appear to be holding my arms, legs or upper body down. *What. . .the. . .fuck.*

I continue to try to shake and pull myself out of this black hole of a chair unsuccessfully.

"GOD DAMN IT!"

I give up in my struggle to break free momentarily, as I sit still and collect my thoughts. I take deep breaths and exhale, in hopes that it'll prevent me from blowing a gasket. Just as I begin to feel calm, my skin starts itching and it feels as if something is crawling on me. This sends me into a panic. I attempt to break free, failing to do so once again.

"WHAT IS HAPPENING TO ME?"

Tears leak from my eyes—all caused by the frustration of feeling trapped. The gasket has blown and I feel my temperature rising. Just as I begin to accept defeat, the laptop on my desk directly in front of me turns on. A video automatically plays. I see the inside of a hotel room. My best friend Scottie is lying on the king-sized bed, naked as the day he was born.

"When you get out the bathroom, I got something I wanna show ya!" Scottie hollers.

I can faintly hear a woman's voice in the background on the tape. Scottie starts to masturbate as he awaits his lady friend.

"Oh my God, Scotty! Is that for me?"

"This is all for you, baby."

The woman walks into sight and my heart drops into the pit of my stomach like a stack of bricks. My wife is also naked and mounts herself onto Scottie's meat. I become nauseous as I watch her pale-white buttocks bounce up and down as she rides his cock. My blood boils and another gasket blows. The veins in my neck nearly rip through the skin as my face gets hot, causing sweat to drip from my pores like an oil leak.

"YOU MOTHERFUCKERS!"

Angie's moans grow louder as the pace of Scottie's strokes speed up.

"NOOOOOOOO," I scream.

I jerk forward and land face first on the floor. The light from the computer screen exposes the army of roaches that are marching all over my body.

"AAAHHHHHHHH!"

I jump to my feet, rapidly brushing my body to rid myself of the unwanted bugs. I rush out of the den and sprint through the dining room. I reach the living room and trip over my own feet, crashing onto the old, dirty carpet. As I lie there, relieved to have escaped the horrors in my den, I hear faint voices from outside.

The front door swings open and the daylight pierces into the damp, dark living room. I rise to my feet. Drawn by the light, I approach the doorway. I look through the screen door and I see my eight-year-old daughter Myra playing jump rope with two other girls. I grab the screen door handle but it shocks me.

"SON OF A—"

I shake my hand in an attempt to wave off the sharp pain of the shock.

"MYRA," I yell. "*MYRA!*"

Myra continues jump-roping with her friends, laughing and smiling as if she can't hear me screaming at the top of my lungs. I bang both my hands against the glass of the screen door but I am thrown backwards by an invisible forcefield. I land on my back but I quickly hop back onto my feet. I charge the screen door once more, just in time to see a white utility van pull up to the curb. Two guys hop out the van wearing ski masks. One of them snatches up Myra and the second guy grabs one of the other girls. The third girl is able to get away, screaming for help as she runs down the sidewalk.

"HELP! HELP. . .I WANT MY DADDY!" Myra screams as the perpetrators team together to get the girls in the van.

"LET MY BABY GO! I'LL FUCKING KILL YOU!" I take several steps backwards, take a deep breath and exhale.

I bolt for the screen door with all my might, drop my shoulder, and then attempt to truck through the door. As soon as my body makes contact with the structure, a powerful force launches me into the air. It slings me twenty feet back and I land in the dining room. I can still hear the sounds of Scottie fucking my wife on tape in my den. I lay on the dining room floor, curl up in the fetal position and bawl my eyes out.

"WHYYY, GOD—WHY! THEY TOOK MY BABY. GOD, PLEASE HELP ME!"

The combination of tears and snot drip down my face. The small amount that doesn't land in my mouth forms a puddle underneath my face. I continue to sob on the floor until I hear footsteps coming down the living room stairs. I wipe my face clean and rise to my feet. I walk into the living room and I see the backside of a woman making her way down the staircase. She's wearing a white down with a tiger lily pattern.

"Angie. . .is that you?" I ask.

Angie reaches the bottom of the stairs and turns to face me. She is deathly pale and her eyes are heavily shadowed by dark bags underneath them. Dried-up tears highlight the corners of her eyes as well. I notice the sides and lower front of her gown are covered in blood. Both her wrists appear to be slit. She stands frozen in place, staring at me blankless.

"Angie...what did you do?"

"You didn't have to kill him, Lyle. Why'd you have to kill him, huh?"

I am baffled with confusion and concern." Kill who, Angie?"

"Scottie, you piece of shit! It wasn't his fault!" Angie screamed. "It's not my fault you'd rather fuck whores than fuck your wife! He made me feel special and you killed him. Murderer!"

Angie charges me with her hands out in an attempt to choke me. *"Murderer!"*

I bat her hands down and pull her close to me, trying my best to restrain her. She continues to fight and resist, so I throw her into the chair nearest us.

"Murderer! Murderer!"

She grabs my face and tries to gouge my eyes out. I free my head from her reach as I continue to keep my hands grasped firmly around her neck. She proceeds with all her strength and energy to strike my face. I squeeze her neck tighter, increasing the pressure I have on her throat.

"Murderer," Angie mutters. She makes an effort to spit in my face but is unable to gather enough saliva to do so.

"I'M NOT A MURDERER!" I scream, sobbing as I tighten my grip around her throat. I close my eyes for a moment. As I open them, I find myself choking a chair pillow. Angie is nowhere to be seen.

"ANNGGGIIIEEEEEE!!" I examine my surroundings. Nothing. She is gone without a trace. I collapse into the chair, sobbing as I hold the pillow for comfort. The Alexa speaker on the fireplace mantle emits an activation beep. I look upwards at the Alexa.

"Daddy..."

"MYRA?"

I jump out of the chair and grab the Alexa speaker from the mantle. "Myra, this is Daddy, baby. Can you hear me?"

"I can hear you, Daddy. It's so cold here. I wanna come home."

"I want you home, baby. God, I miss you so much."

"Why'd you let them take me, Daddy?"

"I'm so sorry, baby. I—I—"

"I yelled for your help and you weren't there, Daddy."

"I know, Myra. I'm sorry. I wish I was there. . .I do."

"But you weren't, were you?" Myra asks, her tone deepening and becoming more aggressive. "Now I'm dead, Daddy—and it's all your fault. It's ALL your fault!"

I become nauseous as the room starts to spin, causing me to become dizzy.

"It's all your fault! It's all your fault!!" Myra screams, becoming a broken record. I stumble through the dining room and walk into my den. The footage of Scottie fucking Angie continues to play. I swoop the laptop up and slam it down on the desk, shattering it into pieces. I can hear Myra continuing to scream at me through the speaker in the living room. I grab my lockbox from the top shelf of the bookcase in my den. I unlock the case and retrieve my revolver. I toss the lockbox to the side and insert the barrel of the gun into my mouth. Myra's voice continues to echo in my mind.

*It's all your fault, Daddy. It's all your fault. . .*

I cock the hammer back and pull the trigger. All sounds cease as I float through complete darkness. The silence is the most peaceful form of solace I could ask for. Just as I begin to appreciate the comfort it brings, I feel what's left of myself being pulled backwards. I use every bit of my energy to try to resist, but I am outmatched. I feel like someone just flushed a toilet and I'm the turd floating down the drain...

*My eyes open to utter darkness. I find myself in my den, sitting in my leather recliner. I must've fallen asleep again. I hate when that happens—because I know my wife will bitch about it later.*

# INCONSIDERATE
## BY KEV NIVEK

It's an awkward thing—to see your roommate masturbating. Exhaling an enormous sigh, James parked his car and turned off the engine. He ducked towards the dash, peeping through his windshield into a second-floor window in his house, hoping his eyes were deceiving him.

They weren't.

Clear as day, a silhouette could be seen in the bathroom shower window, and an arm cranked back and forth like a madman.

"Christ, Ronnie! We talked about this," James mumbled to himself as he grabbed his work bag and then stepped out of the car.

Heading up the porch to the back door, he thought about the conversation his roommates had when they first visited the place. He had mentioned then that he didn't particularly love the translucent shower window. But it wasn't enough of an issue to be a dealbreaker. Today, he found himself wishing it had been.

With yet another sigh, James reached for his keys, hoping to calm himself before he'd inevitably have to look Ronnie in the eyes later. Turning his key in the padlock, he was surprised to not hear a click of the lock. His anger swelled as he reached for the handle and found it unlocked as well.

*Goddamnit, Ronnie!*

Briefly, he kept his outburst to himself, but he was nearing his limit. Closing the door behind him, he was surprised that he was able to kick his shoes off before being pounced on by his loveable puppy, Rockne.

"Rocko, where you at, bud?" he called out, puzzled. It wasn't like the puppy to miss a chance to greet anyone entering the house. James soon walked to the living room, expecting to find a napping dog on one of the couches. *Nope. No doggo. Strike two.*

He hustled up the stairs, fearing the worst. *Did Rockne get out somehow? Was the door not only unlocked but open?* Living on a busy street meant the odds of returning weren't good if Rockne did find a way outside.

As he reached the top of the stairs, he heard Ronnie's music blaring through their shared bathroom door. He turned to open the door to his bedroom, which was right next to the shower. His heart sank as he saw that his playful pup wasn't lying on his bed.

Sadness swam to anger as he realized someone had tossed his room. There were clothes everywhere, as trash littered his bed and countless valuables were on the floor.

*Did someone rob me and steal my damn dog?*

Behind him, James heard the bathroom door open. "Yo, Ronnie. . ..have you seen Rocko, man? I can't find him." He paused for a response, continuing to assess the disaster in front of him. "It's real weird, Ron; I think someone's been in here. My throom ich fuggach hhsscchh..."

James felt an odd sensation as his tongue failed to output his thoughts. Placing a hand on his mouth, he felt the sharp end of a chef's blade sticking out to greet him.

Looking down in absolute panic, James saw nothing but blood. He felt the two halves of his tongue dueling for supremacy as he struggled to call for help. One strong force situated behind James held his arms down as the blade was yanked out from his skull, showering him in his own blood with a sickening squelch.

Flailing forward, he fell to his knees while both of James' hands attempted to hold what was left of his shivved throat together. Convulsing onto his back, he could see a hooded figure standing in the hallway with their back turned. A puddle of blood spilled from the bathroom, brushing against the brown boots of his assailant.

The stocky man looked down at James as he headed for the stairs. Although James could only see the whites of his eyes under the hood, he caught his nonchalant words. . .

"Helluva place you have here."

#  Oh My Love
## By Shawn Baker

My eyes open to a room full of darkness and I find myself in bed alone. I am assuming Bella made her way to the restroom again. She's been sick for the last few days, but refuses to let me take her to the hospital. She is the most hardheaded woman I've ever met, but I wouldn't trade her for the world.

I close my eyes and begin to drift off to sleep when I am awoken by a loud noise. I sit up, staring at the door. Again, I hear a loud thump. I slide on my slippers and make way for the bedroom door. I open it slowly, as my eyes are squinting as they struggle to adjust to the hallway light.

"Bella. . .honey?"

No response.

As I head out into the hallway, an intense uneasiness overwhelms me. I look to my left and see that the bathroom door is open and empty. I hear the TV on in the living room.

"Bella babe?" Again, no response.

I take two more steps down the hallway before I am met by Bella at the end of the hall.

"Feeling any better, baby?" I ask.

She stares at me, eyes dark and hollow.

"Bell--" I'm interrupted by a fierce growl, followed by her charging after me. My instincts kick in and I immediately grab her by the throat. I pin her against the wall.

"BELLA. . .BABE."

I immediately start to cry as I clearly see that the love of my life is gone. She's physically present, but that is it. I stand there—with a hand wrapped tightly around her throat. She continues to stare at me blankly, growling in between attempts to bite me.

I lead her into the bathroom by her throat. Once we're inside, I shove her toward the sink and exit quickly, closing the door with a major sense of urgency. Standing in the hallway, my thoughts overwhelm me to the point where I become lightheaded and start to feel nauseous. Frozen in place, my vision comes back into focus. I then follow the sound of the television.

I find our living room in a disastrous state. The coffee table has been flipped over. Mail, magazines, and various papers are scattered across the floor. The couch and loveseat cushions are ripped. Once my mind processes this chaos, my attention is turned toward the emergency broadcast on the television. The chief of police is being interviewed by a Channel 10 reporter.

"At this point in time, all we know for sure is that bites spread the infection. Stay away from those who are sick. Avoid being bit. We have managed to ship some of them off for testing. We're currently awaiting results from the CDC. In the meantime, my men and I will continue our fight to maintain the outbreak. . ."

I turn the TV off and make my way to the bedroom. I sit on the edge of our bed, distraught as I look at a picture of Bella and I on the day I proposed to her. Considering how fast the world has gone to shit, I've lost damn near all certainty. The only two things I am certain about is that the creature scratching and growling at the bathroom door is no longer the woman I fell in love with, and she will never be that woman again.

After swallowing that tough pill of reality, I rise and walk to the utility closet in the hallway. I grab some rope, two rolls of duct tape, a pillow case, and an aluminum baseball bat. My heart is beating rapidly as I approach the bathroom door. Taking three deep breaths, I proceed to open it. I open it with a push, knocking Bella backwards. I use my bat to sweep her off of her feet. As soon as she falls to the ground, I place my foot on her neck while I cover her head with the pillowcase. I tape the casing around her neck several times. Once secure, I pick her up by the neck and drag her into the bedroom.

Using the rope, I tie her right arm and leg to the upper right bedpost. I repeat this step by doing the same with her left arm and leg to the upper left bedpost. I stand at the end of the bed, staring. I am just completely stupefied by the sight of my "lady."

Snapping out of my state of confusion, I grab my bowie knife out of the bedroom closet. I walk over to the head of the bed, bend down by her ear and whisper, "I love you, Bella." She continues to growl and shake furiously.

I make a clean cut down the side of her night shorts. They slide right off. I take a moment to admire her vagina. I smile as I think about all the times I used to fuck it. I walk over to the dresser and grab the KY jelly out of the top drawer. I take my boxers off and cover my penis with lubricant.

I make way to the bed and get on top of Bella. I rub her chest and abdomen gently with both hands.

"I never thought it'd end like this, Bella Babe. The world as we know it is over. . .but our love will never die."

I kiss each nipple and slowly insert my dick inside of her. I pound away. I ignore her growls of satisfaction for the most part, but occasionally growl back at her. I thrust myself to completion. I lean back slightly on my knees and watch my ejaculation languidly leak from her cold, lifeless body.

I reach over and pick up my bowie knife from the nightstand. I cut the pillowcase off of her head. We stare into each other's eyes briefly.

"Oh, my love."

I caress the side of her face with the back of my hand. I lower myself toward her, allowing Bella to take a bite from my neck. I sit upward, smiling at Bella as blood gushes out of my neck. I fall off the side of the bed. I lay there, back to the floor as I stare at the ceiling. I can't stop smiling as everything fades to black...

# KNOCK, KNOCK
## BY KEV NIVEK

The knife tore through the muscle with a sickening squelch. With a flick of the wrist, Thomas slid the blade along the cutting board. The meat was ice cold under his left palm, leaving his fingers numb. He slid the knife back up the board, lifting his wrist as he pressed down again. The squishing sound nearly emptied his stomach as he held down a gag.

After one final slice, he set the knife down, reaching with both of his hands for the pile of raw meat in front of him. Lifting at arm's length, he plopped it into the bucket with a look of disgust on his face.

Vigorously, Thomas washed his hands, hoping to wash away the awful smell. With a deep breath, he grabbed the bucket and held it under the faucet, calmly waiting for the ice-cold water to rise. Once full he clamped the lid down on the bucket, Thomas grabbed a fresh towel and then set both on the bottom rack of the refrigerator.

***

Jerrold sat alone on the couch—oblivious to his surroundings—while completely entranced by the newest episode of *Tales from the Cosmos*. His eyes were glossy, his stare blank. At this moment, he wasn't Jerrold at all. He was merely a husk, a paperweight. His jaw sat slightly open, enough to drool if it weren't for the cotton-mouth.

The spell was broken by an obnoxiously loud commercial.

"Routs Konda-Hia, home of the—" Jerrold slammed the mute button on his smart table, silencing the shrieking salesman who was shouting at him from the TeleMirror above the mantle. Sliding his finger down the side of the glass tabletop, he turned down the artificial flames on his fireplace heater. Taking a swig from his water pouch, he grabbed two NicoPods from the smart table and stepped toward the front door.

"Where ya headed, bud?" Thomas stood in the entryway of the living room, leaning against the wall. "Is that what I think it is?"

Jerrold's eyes betrayed him as he glanced at the screen with a guilty gulp.

"You fuckin' started without me!" Thomas made a beeline for the remote; Jerrold's slight hesitation would cost him.

"No...come on, man! I'm at the last commercial break. Just let me finish and watch the thing yourself in like ten minutes." Jerrold pleaded his case, now back on the couch, NicoPods clutched in his left hand.

"Hell no; you shouldn't have started without me. You could've helped me prep dinner, but instead, you thought you'd get a little zoned and kicked back. Punishment fits the crime, dude. . . deal with it."

Jerrold huffed as he reached for the bowl. *Might as well take another hit before I step out.*

As he put the pipe up to his lips, a sudden noise startled him. He jumped up in fear, dropping his piece to the ground while spilling precious bits of G onto the carpet.

*BOOM. BOOM. BOOM.*

Three explosive knocks were delivered to the door. Thomas sprang from the couch but didn't immediately head to the door. He paused briefly, giving Jerrold a chance to cover his contraband. Thomas tip-toed to the door, reaching meekly for the deadbolt. Worried, he unlocked it, turning the knob to reveal their visitor.

There was no one there.

Puzzled, Thomas glanced to his left, then quickly back to his right. There was nothing in sight. Tentatively, Thomas tip-toed toward the front porch railing. He silently slid his hands along the rail. Leaning over, he expected to spot a fleeing teen or two gleefully escaping from a successful 'prank.' He was somewhat shocked to find that there was once again nothing to see there.

There was nothing unusual, nothing at all to be seen along the side of his house nor in the abandoned lot next to it. The unreasonably tall grass swayed without effort. Thomas chuckled in confusion and turned away, heading hesitantly to the far side of the porch—where the unclaimed mail of the abandoned half of the duplex was scattered about unceremoniously.

Each step became slower and more methodical as Thomas felt an eerie uncertainty wash over him. Hugging the face of the house, he grabbed the corner tightly, thrusting himself around the edge of the rail.

Scanning the abandoned apartment complex and the chain-link fence that separated him from it, he could see nothing out of the ordinary.

With a defeated sigh, Thomas turned toward the door. Halfway there, he nearly jumped out of his skin upon hearing a rabid rustling to his right.

Tripping over himself, he peeked over the frontside rail along the porch. The bushes were moving as if alive, when a brown ball of fur suddenly darted out and across the yard, bounding boldly to the unkempt yard next door.

"A fucking rabbit?"

Thomas giggled nervously at his previous paranoia. As he reentered the house, he'd completely forgotten about the strange knocks on their door.

"Any luck?" Jerrold handed Thomas a freshly packed bowl upon his inquiry.

"Nope. Nothing out there." Thomas took a long rip from the piece, letting the harsh smoke fill his lungs as he attempted to chase the last few minutes from his mind. He held the smoke in as he passed the piece back to Jerrold. Turning to lock the door, Thomas again hopped in fear when he heard the revolving of the auto locks, whirring and spinning quickly to lock the front door.

"What the hell, man?" He looked crossly at Jerrold, who shrugged in innocent confusion. "Is the Auto-Lock turned on? I thought you disabled it."

Jerrold jumped up and ran his fingers along the edge of the table, pulling up the Home Settings menu. Flicking his wrist until he found the Security section. Upon opening the tab, his eyebrows raised as they could both see that the Auto-Lock feature was turned off.

Thomas rounded the table and took a seat next to Jerrold, sparking the bowl again as he stared down his unruly front door.

*BOOM. BOOM. BOOM.*

Thomas dropped the bowl, cough-spitting all over himself as the cherry began to burn a hole in the carpet floor.

"Can we please not spill *all* of my Glow on the floor today?" Jerrold scolded as he bent down in an effort to retrieve his fallen comrade.

Thomas rushed for the door this time, determined to catch this prankster in the act. He struggled momentarily with the locks, which seemed slightly heavier than before. Swinging the handle as hard as he could, Thomas tore out of the front door and onto the porch. He ran to his right, hoping that a change in strategy would help him find his tormentor.

Without fear, he whipped around the corner, quickly assessing the area before heading back to the left side of the house. Again, he found nothing. Gazing longingly into the tall grass, he thought he saw movement but convinced himself that he wouldn't be tricked by the same rabbit twice. Defeated, he ducked back inside.

He had barely closed the front door behind him when another loud knock echoed through the house.

*BOOM. BOOM. BOOM.*

Horrified, Thomas and Jerrold stared at each other. Without a word, Thomas pounced into action, sprinting through the living and dining rooms, well on his way to the kitchen's back door.

"Oswald, lock the front door," Thomas spat into the implant on his left wrist as he hustled forward. The house's smart software obliged him as he could hear the locks swiveling into place even as he approached the back door.

Twisting the knob on the already unlocked back door, he hopped out to the back patio, intent to end this once and for all. He slammed the door behind him as he pounded down the stairs.

He stopped dead in his tracks as he heard the feverish whirring of the back door locking itself behind him.

Forgetting his cause, he leaped back up the porch, desperately fumbling with his keys as he cussed at his padlock.

"Oswald! Open up, man, it's me!" Dropping his keys as he yelled into his implant, the door held firm.

"Oswald! What the fuck. . .open up! Password 4293; unlock the back door, damnit!"

He wrestled again with the handle but was once again denied.

"Fuckin' A, Oswald!" Thomas kicked the door in defiance, falling back as he bounced off the immovable door. *Goddamned fuckin' stupid ass 'SmartTek.'*

Thomas gathered himself and his keys, taking a quick yet deep breath as he unlocked the back padlock and jumped inside.

*CRAAACKK*

An explosion of pain hit Thomas in the forehead as he crashed into the still-open doorway. Warm blood trickled down his face; it streamed between his eyes, along the edge of each nostril. He instinctively threw his arms over his head, partially blocking the next blow.

"Jerr! Help me, man—please!" Thomas yelped as he braced himself for another blow. After a few seconds without one, he peeked through his forearms to see a heavily panting and sweaty Jerrold holding a large wrench.

"I'm sorry, Tom. . .I thought you were a burglar." Jerrold dropped the wrench at his feet and rushed to help his friend.

"Goddamnit! That really fuckin' hurts, you dick." Thomas scolded his friend even as Jerrold helped him up from the floor and locked the door behind them.

They hadn't made it past the basement door when they felt three more blasts rattle their walls.

*BOOM. BOOM. BOOM.*

The roommates stared at each other in disbelief. This time, the knocks seemed to come from upstairs.

*BOOM. BOOM. BOOM.*

"What the hell is going on, Thomas? Who was that outside?" Jerrold let go of his friend and began to pace around the kitchen floor.

"I don't have a fucking clue; there wasn't anyone outside. The stupid house locked me out!" Thomas had fallen back onto the wall, leaning heavily against it for balance.

*BOOM. BOOM. BOOM.*

"Well, I don't think the house is doing that! What the hell should we do, man; call the cops?" Jerrold was nearly running in a circle at this point, his hands planted firmly on his head as he squeezed his temples with his fists.

"Calm down and grab that wrench. We can't call the cops so get your shit together and help me up the stairs." Thomas slid along the wall toward the stairway and popped through the walkway over to the stairway railing.

Jerrold wasn't far behind, lugging Thomas up the stairs with his right arm, wielding the wrench in his left.

*BOOM. BOOM. BOOM.*

The knocks appeared to intensify the closer they got to the top of the stairs.

*BOOM. BOOM. BOOM.*

With only three steps to go, Jerrold propped Thomas against the railing and handed him the wrench.

"Stay here. . .I'll be right back." Jerrold ducked into his bedroom door at the right of the stairs. To the left, the attic door was quaking.

*BOOM. BOOM. BOOM.*

A moment later, Jerrold returned, brandishing a silver-handled VK-7 laser pistol.

"Holy shit, how long have you had that?!" Thomas retreated into the wall as Jerrold reached out to him. The pace of the knocking increased.

*BOOM. BOOM. BOOM.*

*BOOM. BOOM. BOOM.*

"Come on. . .now's not the time." Jerrold grabbed Thomas as they crept up the final stairs and turned left down the hall toward the attic door at the end. It shook and rattled from frame to floor each time the knocks occurred, staring blankly at them whenever it stopped.

Slowly stepping forward, Jerrold and Thomas braved themselves for whatever horror awaited them on the other side of that door.

*BOOM. BOOM. BOOM.*

*BOOM. BOOM. BOOM.*

*BOOM. BOOM. BOOM.*

With a synchronized sigh, they stopped in front of the door. Suddenly, the knocking stopped.

They stood there for a moment, an arm's length from the door. Unable to believe that this had been a figment of their collective imagination, they both found themselves hoping to hear the knocking return.

"Go ahead; get it over with." Thomas nudged Jerrold as he leaned against the wall in the hallway.

"Why m—" Jerrold began to protest, but after taking a quick glance at his friend's bleeding head, he decided against it. With another deep breath, he reached for the door handle. Behind him, Thomas shifted his weight in an attempted attack mode—his wrench ready to wreak havoc on the intruder.

*ERRRRRCCCKK*

The door creaked as Jerrold swung it open, jumping back with the pistol aimed at the empty attic stairs. Hand shaking, Jerrold held his aim as best as he could while approaching the attic steps. With a groan, Thomas trudged forward beside him as they reached the stairs at the same time. Jerrold took the lead with Thomas quickly falling a few steps behind. Upon reaching the middle landing of the stairway, Jerrold completely froze, nearly dropping his blaster in the process.

*BOOM. BOOM. BOOM.*

Somewhere up those stairs, the knocking had begun anew.

*BOOM. BOOM. BOOM.*

*BOOM. BOOM. BOOM.*

Jerrold turned to grab Thomas, throwing him up the final few steps. Across the room, a portion of the wall was shaking.

*BOOM. BOOM. BOOM.*

*BOOM. BOOM. BOOM.*

"Hu—who's there? Show yourself!" Jerrold stammered as they tread lightly forward, inching their way to the rocking wall.

*BOOM. BOOM. BOOM.*

*BOOM. BOOM. BOOM.*

*BOOM. BOOM. BOOM.*

As they approached the wall, it then fell silent. Again they stood entranced, mesmerized by the phenomena they'd found themselves surrounded by. They stood staring at the wall, drenched in fear and sweat—yet standing in awe—patiently awaiting their fate. It was Thomas who reached out first. His eyes had a glaze to them as he stared, fixated on a spot in the paint that looked to be pulsating as if the wall itself were breathing.

*CRRAAAAASSSHH*

An undeniable force shot the wall forward, crushing Thomas beneath it with a sickening thud. Jerrold fled immediately, wasting no time to check on the status of his friend, nor see what it was that was chasing him. As he reached the top of the steps, he thought he heard the slurping sounds of something eating at his friend's flesh.

With a leap, he flew over the steps, crashing down on the landing and dropping his blaster. He looked for it momentarily but left it behind as he jumped the last half of the steps, certain he could hear footsteps thundering toward the stairs above him.

Sprinting down the hall, Jerrold felt a sharp pain shoot up his left leg. One of those landings had done a number on this ankle. He fought through the pain as he turned toward the second-story steps, sliding down the railing to avoid putting pressure on his leg.

Halfway down the stairs, he was stunned to see his front door hanging wide open. Grabbing the rail in front of him, Jerrold launched himself over the side of the steps, landing softly on the couch below. As he bounced up, bounding for the door, it suddenly swung itself shut, whirring and revving as it locked in front of him.

"Oh, fuck me." An exhausted Jerrold focused on the dining room, limping past the stairway as he heard the crash of the attic door swinging into the wall, followed by galloping footsteps above him.

Passing the stairs into the kitchen, he saw that the back door now hung wide open. He could not afford to hesitate, but his gut told him this too would be a trap. After two more steps, the door slammed shut, locking itself as he was already turning from it. He could hear the thunderous stomps getting closer, barreling down the steps.

As he turned to run for the kitchen window, he heard the basement door swing open with a crash behind him.

*AAAIIIRRRGGEEHH*

He had no time to turn and face his demise. With a shriek, his world went black.

# MISTEE & ME

## BY SHAWN BAKER

I sit near the window, watching the trees pass as the school bus makes its way through the neighborhood. My headphones rest along my ears, pumping out Greta Van Fleet as we ride along the route. We stop at the end of a cul-de-sac and drop off a few students. Thank God it's Friday. This week has been brutal. Trigonometry is kicking my ass.

Ms. Betty, the bus driver, pulls up to Steve Gomey's house. This is one of my favorite stops because it means my stop is next. Steve brushes past my seat and scurries off the bus. Ms. Betty closes the door behind him and drives off. I stand up to stretch and I notice a petite, raven- haired beauty sitting at the back of the bus. She's wearing glasses with a thick, black frame and has a small mole planted on her left cheek. I contemplate whether I should approach her. We're the last two students on the bus and this seems like a golden opportunity to make a move.

I grab my backpack and stroll to the back of the bus. I sit down in the seat directly to her right and I throw my bag to the side. We make eye contact and she flashes me a smile. I return it with a smile of my own. "Hi. I'm Jake."

"Mistee," she replies.

"I don't remember ever seeing you on this route before."

"Yeah. . .this is my first day. My family just moved here from Florida."

"Nice. What brought you guys to Ohio?"

"My dad's job. He's in the military."

"Oh, okay. Military brat—I can dig it."

"Yeah..." Mistee says before we both chuckle. "So what do you do for fun around here?" she then asks.

"Absolutely nothing. Welcome to New Knavish!"

We share laughter and I think I just fell in love. Her smile is captivating. The shape of her narrow, yet juicy lips tickles my soul.

"Wanna hang out later? My parents are gone for the weekend. I have the house all to myself."

I am stunned. My mouth feels frozen. I know what I want to say. My obvious response is hell yes, but I simply can't spit it out. "Well. . .?"

"Sure. That'd be cool."

She grins. I know she can sense that that was my weak attempt at trying to be nonchalant. A girl like Mistee can see through any facade. The bus comes to a halt and the front doors swing open.

"Damn, this is my stop. Shit..." I fiddle through my pockets to grab my cell phone. I can't seem to find it quickly enough.

"Home sweet home, Jake. Let's go!" Ms. Betty hollers from the driver's seat, her eyes leering back at me through the rearview mirror.

"One sec!" I holler back.

"Here," says Mistee, pulling out a black marker from her notebook and grabbing my left hand. She proceeds to write her address on my hand. "I don't have a cell phone. Just stop by later after eight."

"I sure will." We exchange smiles as I rise to my feet and exit the bus. I get off at the corner of Massing and Edgerton. I start hoofing it home, but I can't stop looking at my hand. I listen to "This Magic Moment" by The Drifters as I walk down Edgerton. I keep envisioning her warm, inviting smile. It just sucked me in like a vacuum. *My own little, personal Dirt Devil.*

I reach my house and step inside. I run upstairs to my room and shut the door. I immediately write her address down on a blank piece of paper from my binder. I undress myself completely and stand in front of the mirror. I examine my penis and lightly pull on it a couple of times. Maybe I'm hoping it'll grow a little bit more with each tug. Knowing what I need to do, I stretch out on my bed and grab the lotion from my bedside table. I squirt about a quarter-sized amount onto my right hand. I place the lotion back into the drawer and I grab my "happy cloth." I rub the lotion onto my penis and begin to stroke myself. My attention alternates between the address on my left palm and fantasies of rubbing skins with Tesla. I jerk myself until I blow my load into the cloth. I use the dry side to clean myself up, then proceed to the shower.

✻ ✻ ✻

It's a quarter after seven and my nerves are kicking in. I double-up on deodorant, brush my teeth, and follow it up with some mouthwash. I make my way to the closet and grab my polo top with the least amount of wrinkles. *Dress for success* as my dad would say. I finish dressing and head out the door.

I bike my way uphill, passing the defunct New Knavish Sanitarium on my left. I quickly pedal past it, trying not to look at the deteriorated building. Just seeing the place gives me the willies. I bust a left on Crawford Drive and turn my focus to reading the house numbers. I let off the pedals as I coast in the dirt driveway. *233. . .235. . .boom.* I pull into the dirt driveway at 237 and I take it all the way back. I see Mistee standing in the doorway of a small guesthouse behind her house. I release the kickstand on my bike and park it.

"Any trouble finding the place?" Mistee wonders.

"Not at all. My Aunt used to stay in this part of town."

"Awesome. Come on in. This is where I hang out."

I enter the shed to find that it's much more spacious than it looks from the outside. There's a beige leather couch to my left. A floor-model big screen TV is along the wall opposite the doorway. Mistee goes to the couch and I follow. We sit side by side. She places her hand on my knee and flashes a smile.

"Don't be nervous," she softly says.

*Easier said than done.* Sweat puddles have formed in the palms of my hands. I've never had sex with a girl— let alone be in the position to do so. I try to gather my thoughts and think of something cool to say.

"This is a nice place you have here."

Mistee stares at me expressionless, then leans in for a kiss. I try to match her lip movement stride for stride. Feeling courageous, I slide my tongue into her mouth. I'm surprised at how dry her mouth is. Not what I was expecting at all. She pulls my shirt off and pummels me into the couch. She removes her shirt as well and throws it on the floor. She grabs both of my hands and places them on her breasts. She moans as she dry-rides me. Suddenly, a boom box atop the TV starts playing 90s grunge music.

"What the..."

"Shhh," Mistee whispers, placing her pointer finger on my lips. She gets off of me. *Damn, I ruined it.* She takes her pants off, becoming completely naked. I get up and follow suit. She lays down on the couch and I lay on top of her.

"I know I probably shouldn't tell you this. . ." I pause. "But I'm a. . .you know?"

"A virgin?"

"Yeah. . .that."

"It's okay. Me too."

"Really?"

Mistee pulls me in for a kiss. As we're swapping tongues, I gently slide my penis into her vagina. It is damp and cold. Ignoring this surprise, I close my eyes as I continue to rock my hips back and forth, moaning with delight at each thrust. I open my eyes to find Mistee staring through me, with a stern facial expression. She doesn't seem to be enjoying it nearly as much as me but what the hell, *I'm doing it!* She digs both her hands into my back and her eyes change from brown to red for a quick moment—just in time for me to finish inside of her. Unfazed and still erect, I continue to pound away.

It feels like hours have gone by, but I'm finally running out of fuel. I ejaculate for the fourth time and lay on Mistee. I rest my head along her chest but I can't hear her heartbeat over the same damn Nirvana song that has been on repeat the whole time. I sigh out in joy and love juices. Mistee lies there in silence.

"Thank you," I say.

"It's getting late. You should go."

"Sure. . .you okay?"

"Yep."

I get off of her and start putting my clothes on. She doesn't move, only staring at the ceiling. I finish getting dressed and lean down to kiss her goodbye. She doesn't return the kiss.

"I'll see ya later," I say with uncertainty. I doubt she ever wants to see me again.

"Bye."

I exit the shed, hop on my bike and then head home.

***

I countdown the hours at school, looking forward to seeing Mistee on the bus ride home. The last bell rings and all the students make their way out to the bus lot at the south entrance of the building. I board the bus and take my usual seat, opting for the aisle side instead of the window. I patiently await Mistee's arrival, but it doesn't happen. Ms. Betty pulls out of the lot and begins the route.

When I get home, I drop my backpack off before hopping on my bike. I make my way to Tesla's house. I coast down Crawford Drive. I arrive at her address, but....*what the shit?* This can't be right. The house looks nothing like before and there isn't a guest house in the back either. All I see is an old rundown shed with peeling green paint. I park my bike in front of the house and walk to the front door. I knock three times. An elderly man with rotting teeth opens the door. The stench of mold and cat piss invade my nostrils immediately.

"Is Mistee home?"

"Who??" barks the old man.

"Mistee!" I reply.

"Don't no Mistee live here, boy."

"But I was just here with her Friday night."

"I don't know how to break it to ya, son, but no girl named Mistee lives here. There hasn't been a girl your age living here in since ninety-eight."

"Honestly?"

"Yeah, buddy. The Richards who lived here had a girl about your age. Though she died in the fire."

"A *fire?*"

"Burnt the whole damn shed down. Killed her and three of her friends. Unfortunate, but that's why we were able to get this place so cheap. Property's a lot cheaper when people die. Especially kids, ya see?"

Unsure of what to say, I stand frozen in place. My brain feels like it's about to explode from the difficulty of trying to process this information.

"Actually, wait one second!" says the elderly man. He disappears into the house, returning with a newspaper clipping eventually. "Here it is."

The man shows me an old copy of the New Knavish Courier. The obituary is clear as day. *Mistee Pagen, 15.* The picture is an identical match to the beautiful girl I performed coitus with the night before. My face reddens and sweat drips from my pores. A mixture of confusion and embarrassment flow through my mind. How could this be? I know for a fact I ejaculated into *someone* multiple times last night. Is it possible I had sex with a *ghost?*

"You all right, young fella?"

*HELL NO I'M NOT* is what I want to say. How would you feel if you had sex with the spirit of a dead chick? I don't think you'd be into it, old man.

I soon collect myself. "Yeah. . .I'm gonna go now. Thank you."

I quickly exit the porch, hop on my bike and fly out of there like a bat out of hell. I pedal as fast as I can, refusing to look back at the place where I lost my virginity to the most wondrous entity I'd ever seen. Wait...I did *lose* my virginity, right? Do ghosts count? Damn. . .well, it...*what the shit.*

# IN THE ZONE
## BY KEV NIVEK

Fingers pummeled the Holotablet. Young Atin was dialed in; those two Aiderrals he bought from Xeke were working wonders. This final research thesis was flying, practically fleeing from him. He turned the corner and headed for conclusion avenue, finishing the paper only minutes later.

Pleased with himself, Atin stretched from his chair and strode toward the kitchen to prepare a celebratory drink. Leaving his room, he was surprised to find that the kitchen light was the only one on.

*Lipe and Xeke must be upstairs blasting Commie Zombies. They'd better not beat it without me.*

Undaunted, Atin rushed into the kitchen and grabbed a glass. Filling it with ice, he reached above the fridge for his favorite bottle of scotch. On the tips of his toes, he glanced above his shoulder, agitated that his precious vice had not yet met his hand. Without hesitation, he sped through the dark until he reached the bottom of the steps.

"Hey, Xeke. You got my bottle up there, man? Your boy needs his medicine!" Atin waited patiently for a moment, but the silence changed his tune.

He walked up a few steps before shouting into the darkness above. "Lipe! You up there? You and Xeke better have some of that juice up there with you!" His words echoed up the hall, but again, his words were met with silence. A slight chill ran up Atin's spine as he made his way back down the stairs.

Turning to the light, he stumbled his way through the dining room. His legs were losing strength as his head began to ache.

*Fuckin' Xeke. What's in these things?* He dropped the glass of melted ice on the counter before leaning heavily onto it himself.

The warm kitchen light was soothing. The cool breeze was a peaceful contrast. He took a long, deep breath of fresh air. After another gulp, Atin turned from the counter. Suddenly, he froze, his eyes bulging in horror. The kitchen window had been shattered.

Atin looked up in shock as the light above him burned brighter. The floating orb seemed to be closing in. Atin tried to shield his eyes, but despite his greatest effort, he couldn't move his arm. The light was blinding now, accompanied by a wave of calm that reached his core. He could no longer feel the ground beneath his feet.

Weightless, he felt a rush of euphoria as the light absorbed him completely.

*CRACK*

In an instant, the metallic orb blasted through the remnants of the window. Hurtling toward the nearby forest, it stopped momentarily. Hovering above the trees, it vibrated violently until blasting into the atmosphere.

# SWEET DREAMS
## BY SHAWN BAKER

Her soft ivory skin illuminated under the moonlight as she made her way up the hill. As I followed behind, I couldn't seem to shake her scent. The smell of Coco Chanel invaded my nostrils. So strong that I could damn near taste it. Every time she turned her head and smiled at me, I felt free. A rush of excitement struck my body like a bolt of lightning. For a guy who rarely smiles, there was no way to not smile back at her. Truth be told, my face was beginning to hurt from it.

"Keep up, Jerry! We're almost there," she said.

"I'm coming," I replied.

There she goes with another gorgeous smile. Here I go, returning one back. I just met this girl, but I swear I'm falling for her already.

As we approached the cabin at the top of the hill, butterflies filled my stomach. My nerves were screaming. *Don't mess this up! Be cool! Chill, man. . .chill.*

I stepped onto the porch as she opened the door. She turned to me and flashed that gorgeous smile.

"Are you ready?" she asks.

It was as if my tongue had gone numb from excitement. My mouth would not respond. The words *'hell yes'* were clear as day in my mind, but refused to be spoken. The silence lasted long enough for her to assume I was. She looked me in the eyes, smiling as if she could read my mind.

"Well, come on then."

She grabbed me by the hand and led me into the cabin. The interior was nothing like I expected. Based on the solitary location, I was under the impression that it may be an abandoned property. Not the case at all. The place reeked of Pine Sol and not a spot of dust could be found. Flames crackled in the fireplace. A bottle of Chardonnay on ice rested alongside two wine glasses on the coffee table near the fireplace. It was obvious that she had prepared for this encounter. I must say, I really liked her style.

We made our way to the sofa. We sat down and soaked up the warmth from the fire. I reached out for the wine when she grabbed my hand. We stared into each other's eyes briefly before our lips connected magnetically. Our tongues brushed against each other's while we passionately massaged each other's backs. That led to her unzipping my pants, revealing a fully erect penis.  She placed her mouth on it and sucked it while I fingered her vagina. Before I knew it, my pants were off and she was mounting my lap. She lifted her nightgown up just a tad before sliding onto my shaft. She rode me ferociously. It took every random thought I could possibly think of to keep myself from coming too soon. I flipped her on her back and started thrusting inside of her. She placed her left hand on the back of my head in an attempt to bring it closer. She leaned in and whispered in my ear, "Glad you were able to make it, Jerry."

"Jerry. . .Jerry. . .JERRY!"

I woke up to the sound of my girlfriend Eileen yelling at me.

"What, Eileen?"

"Are you getting up?"

"What does it look like?"

"It looks like you overslept about a half hour."

"Oh shit! Are you serious?"

I quickly sit up on the edge of the bed. The alarm clock reads 8:34 a.m.

"Damn it, Eileen. How come you're just now waking me up?"

"I was in the shower. You're a grown man. I didn't think I needed to make sure you were up on time."

"You know what, Eileen? You better watch that dirty little mouth of yours before I fuck it."

There is a brief silence, followed by us both laughing.

"You're crazy, Jerry," said Eileen.

"I know, I know," I replied.

Eileen went back into the master bathroom. I followed. She was standing in front of the sink brushing her teeth. I walked up behind her and wrapped my arms around her. I started to kiss her neck. She let out a soft, satisfactory moan.

"Jerry, you got to go to work."

"I am already late, babe. What difference is an extra fifteen minutes gonna make?"

I continued to kiss her neck, working my way up to her right earlobe. I gave it a little nibble.

"Okay. . .but let's make it quick. My sister's waiting on me to take her to meet the wedding planner."

"You got it, babe," I said.

A couple of weeks had gone by and I slept dreamlessly every night. I'd lie down each night with the hopes of running into my dream vixen. It never happened. Eileen and I have been together for almost two years now. We have had our ups and downs, but the ship has sailed smoothly for the most part. I almost feel guilty for *wanting* to sleep with another woman in my dreams, but it *is a dream* after all.

I finally cleaned out the first floor utility closet in our apartment. I found a box of my grandfather's belongings that I'd been looking for. He passed last April. This box of old war medals and gold coins is the only thing I have of his. I was fortunate enough to land some photos of him and I from when I was a child as well. As I'm strolling down memory lane, I hear a car pull into the driveway. I look out the blind to see that it is Eileen. She enters the apartment in tears.

"What's wrong, babe?" I ask.

"Is there something you want to tell me, Jerry?"

"No...I mean, I cleaned out the utility closet today."

"No, Jerry! I mean do you want to tell me who you've been fucking!?!"

"What the fuck are you talking about, Eileen?"

"I had a follow up appointment with Dr. Holloway today."

"Yeah. . .and?"

"Well, I was hoping you could explain to me how I have fucking chlamydia, Jerry!"

"I don't know, Eileen. That sounds like a question you could answer yourself. Who have you been fucking?"

"Just you, you sorry piece of shit!"

"Fuck off, Eileen! I know damn well where my dick has been! You are the only woman I have been with in real life."

"What the fuck does that mean? Real life?"

# Alligator Sweatpants

"Look. . .I had a dream a couple of weeks back where I had sex with a woman, but IT WAS ONLY A DREAM! So before you get even more bent out of shape, just let the fact that IT WAS A DREAM sink in a bit."

"So wait a minute. . .you expect me to sit here and believe that some bitch in a dream gave you chlamydia? How fucking stupid do you think I am, Jerry?"

"I don't think you're stupid, Eileen! I am telling you the damn truth, though. Maybe there is something you aren't telling me?"

"I have no reason to lie to you, Jerry. I wouldn't be freaking out on you like this if there was another person I could've gotten it from."

We both sat and endured an awkward silence.

"You know what," said Eileen after a bit. "I'm gonna stay at my Mom's for a while."

"What the fuck, Eileen! I swear I am telling you the truth. Please..."

"I am sorry, Jerry, but I don't believe you. I CAN'T believe you."

Eileen rose to her feet and headed to the bedroom to pack. I sat in the recliner, completely blown away by the current events. I dreaded every moment I sat there, alone with my thoughts.

*How could this have happened? There is NO WAY I could have caught it from the lady in my dream. Right? Eileen is full of shit! She knows she fucked somebody else. Probably that nerd from her job. I have seen the way he looks at her. Fuck that guy! This is some bullshit! Please don't leave, Eileen. . .please, baby. There has to be a reasonable explanation for all this. Yeah, you fucked another dude! There it is! No, she'd never do that to me. WHAT THE FUCK IS HAPPENING!?!?!*

I heard the bedroom door close upstairs and the sound of footsteps. Eileen came downstairs with her suitcase and a duffle bag full.

"I am just taking my clothes and the essentials I need. I am leaving everything else. I will be at my Mom's. I love you, Jerry.

She began to choke up, trying her hardest to fight back the tears.

"I just can't trust you anymore. I can't continue to live a lie. I wish you the best."

"Eileen. . .babe."

"Bye, Jerry."

She leaned down to kiss me on the forehead and then exited promptly. And just like that, she was gone.

I continued to sit in the recliner, devastated by what had just happened. I love Eileen. I never would have cheated on her. My sadness quickly turned to anger, then back to sadness. I was a mess. I made my way to the kitchen. I poured myself a whiskey and coke— strong on the whiskey. I drank the whole glass before I even left the kitchen. So I made another. . .and another.

I plopped back down in the recliner. I took my phone off the charger. No missed calls or notifications. I turned the ringer on silent. I didn't want to be bothered for the rest of the night. Yawning, I turned on the TV and started scrolling through Netflix. I settled on a movie that looked like it may have quite a bit of violence in it. Violence is good. I feel my eyes getting heavy. I have been fighting sleep, but it's a fight I am bound to lose. I lie here, thinking of Eileen. Even more, I can't stop thinking about the lady in my dream. Maybe it's a good thing Eileen left. Everything happens for a reason, right?

*Her soft ivory skin illuminated under the moonlight as she made her way up the hill...*

# THE MORNING AFTER
## BY KEV NIVEK

Iwake up to the chilly sensation that can only be experienced after a night of sleeping drenched in your own sweat. I've had the dream every night for the past 15 months, and not once has the vividness of these awful images dimmed in my mind's eye.

I close my eyes and sit up. Head resting on my forearms, I take deep breaths until my heartbeat slows and my mind clears. I have no idea how long this will take, but it seems to me that it takes a little longer every day.

Once calm, my senses begin to function again and I'm reminded of the cold puddle I am sitting in, which I'm now certain cannot be sweat. Upon opening my eyes, my calm state is obliterated with a mortar shell of panic and then a somber realization. The chill that crawls up my spine makes this morning's prior one feel like a cool breeze.

I am sharing this sweat- and piss-riddled bed with the corpse of what was once a beautiful young woman; her body's taut yet twisted, like some kind of warped two-by-four.

The next thing I know, I'm up to my chin in porcelain, every foul fluid I have spewing from my mouth with the viciousness of a geyser. There is neither a tear left in my eyes nor any mucus left in my nose. Rather, it has all gathered on my face and my hands.

I decide that the tub's the best place to clean myself off.

What a bad idea.

An unforeseen round two erupts from my esophagus and lands with a splash at the bottom of the tub. *Great. . .as if I haven't made a big enough mess here already.*

I clean myself off and venture out into the common area of the apartment to see if any of her roommates are awake. I doubt anyone slept through the guttural performance I just put on in the restroom. I scan the living and dining rooms quickly—as they're technically the same room. I walk into the kitchen.

*All clear. . .*

My heart is seemingly trying to escape my chest, and its rampant beating is only worsened by what my eyes unveil next.

Three doors are in front of me now: her room, the bathroom, and one last unanswered question at the end of the hall.

By the time I reach the door, my palms are saturated. I reach for the knob slowly. The sun shines in from her bedroom window on my right, reflecting light on the doorknob and my glistening left hand alike. A stagnant wave of putrid air wafts in from the bed. I almost throw up yet again.

I reel in a deep breath, grab the handle, and yank the door open. I'm instantly hit in the face by some flying object.

*Shit!*

My eyes well up with more tears that I don't want but can't control. Mucus has announced its return to my nose and is leaking down to my mouth. Whatever the hell that was just hit me square in the eye. Momentarily disoriented, I still manage to get my non-throbbing right eye open enough to see the face of my object-tossing adversary. I'm startled into laughter by what I see.

It's a closet.

Nothing but a damned linen closet. I must've opened the door too quickly, causing a belt to fly off the hook on the inside of the door and hit me in the face. I stare at the belt on the floor and shake my head.

My breathing slows down and with that, my brain appears to have returned from its brief hiatus.

I now have some time. This is good. I need time right now like a man on death row needs it, and if I don't put my time to good use, that's exactly where I'll end up.

No need to try and search for clues of my innocence. I have no idea what happened here last night, but innocent or not, I'm certain I don't want to be around to plead my case with the detectives. Guilt sinks into my stomach like a rock. What the hell happened? Could I have done this? Maybe in my blacked-out state, my drunken subconscious did what I would never do. Maybe I'm one of those monsters you hear about, quietly waiting to reveal itself. Maybe I've been set up.

. .

Maybe, maybe, maybe.

I groan. Such thoughts are a waste of my time. I cannot solve the "whodunit" mystery; what I need to remember is where I went. Who was with me? Who saw the two of us together last night? My hand has been forced. I must cover all my tracks and determine whether there's any way to buy myself some more time.

I'm no fool; there is only one possible outcome for this confusing story, and it features me sitting in a human bug zapper.

*Time. I've gotta find a way to give myself even more of it.* I frantically search her room for evidence of my presence. I don't find any, but I don't have a forensics kit handy either. Hustling back to the kitchen, I find some ammonia and bleach under the sink. I carry both with me back to her room, unsure of which to use but somewhat certain that I've seen one used to clean up a crime scene in a movie before.

As I unscrew the ammonia bottle, a series of beeps startles me, causing the bottle to escape my grasp. I quickly scoop the emptying bottle from the floor before searching for the source of the sound. The pace of the beeps increases as I crawl to her nightstand. Her phone lies right next to it, placed near her head underneath the bed.

The blue light of the screen flickers with every new sound. Hastily, I grab a handful of tissues before using them to inspect the phone further.

An icon on the screen informs me that it's only 7:10 in the morning. *Why's her phone blowing up so early?* I can't see any of the messages, but they are all from a guy named Jack.

*Shit, shit.*

I'm pacing the room once more; I've no idea of what to do.

*Screw it. Back to the plan.*

I dump the bleach and the remaining ammonia in the bathroom. I wipe every accessible surface in a matter of minutes, bringing the tissues with me as I then exit the front door. I concentrate on looking casual as I head down the stairs.

But upon entering the lobby, I stop dead in my tracks.

In my mystified state, I didn't even hear the sirens. As the cruisers surround the entrance, their authoritative sound becomes deafening.

# Fetish Friendly

## by Shawn Baker

Lyle sat eagerly in his car, searching for the perfect match. He scrolled through the feed on his phone, reading the caption of each post. It was two o' clock in the morning and the thirst was strong. With one hand holding his cell phone, the other rubbed his flaccid penis through his jeans. He must have viewed a hundred posts, but was left unfulfilled. Each profile was more unsatisfactory than the one before.

Just when he thought the cause was lost, he stumbled across the perfect mate. The caption brought a smile to his face and joy to his eyes.

CUM MEET YOUR DESTINY! 27 SWF FF
THICK IN ALL THE RIGHT PLACES
AIM TO PLEASE AND AIM WELL

Under the caption were three pictures of a Caucasian woman with long, jet black hair. Her septum was pierced and she had tattoo sleeves on each arm. She also had a lipstick print tattooed on her right buttocks. Each picture was revealing. All three had her performing provocative poses. Lyle's favorite showed her bent over a bed—her whole ass facing the camera—as she looked back smiling.

Lyle quickly clicked on the *View Full Profile* tab. He copied and pasted the number listed in her bio and entered it into the dialer. He sat patiently as the line rang. He shivered with excitement as the ringing ceased and a female's voice greeted him on the other end.

"Hello," said the female.

"Is this Destiny?" Lyle asked.

"Depends on who's asking," said the female, in a sweet, jokily tone.

Lyle paused briefly with confusion, not picking up on the sarcasm. "Uhh, this is Lyle. I saw your profile on LinkUp."

"Oh. Well. . .hello, Lyle. This is Destiny."

Lyle fist pumped jubilantly, nearly knocking the white and fuzzy dice off of the rearview mirror. He held the phone away from his face as he took two deep breaths in an attempt to regain composure.

"Still there, sweetie?" Destiny asked.

"Yes! Hell yes," Lyle replied.

"Good. Thought I lost you for a sec."

"Nope. I'm still here."

"So. . .how are you?" Destiny asked with innocence.

"I'd be a lot better if I was with you."

"Oh yeah? Well, get over here."

"You betcha. What's your address?"

"The Franklinton on Whittier. Room two-six-five."

"Got it. I will be there in about fifteen minutes."

"Better be."

"I will. See you soon, beautiful."

"See ya."

***

Lyle pulled into the motel parking lot and took a spot near the south entrance. He exited his vehicle with a rose in hand and made his way up the outside stairs. The second-floor balcony reeked of crack smoke and wet dog. He scurried along, ignoring the attempts from junkies asking for change against the rail. As he passed room 261, a scrawny woman wearing a dingy white nightgown stood barefoot in the doorway, nodding off and on. Just as she seemed to be completely dead to the world, she snapped out of her trance and looked at Lyle with deep confusion.

"I ain't got no fucking pudding," barked the woman.

Lyle was caught off guard by the woman's distraught demeanor and chose to keep walking forward. He heard the door slam shut behind him. Two rooms down lied his destination. Butterflies fluttered his stomach as he approached the door. He reached for the crimson red door and knocked three times, each knock slightly louder than the last. Only seconds passed before the door swung open and he was greeted by the face of an angel.

Destiny's long black hair hung past her shoulders and contrasted perfectly against her pale white skin. She was wearing red lipstick and black mascara. She answered the door wearing nothing but a black bra and panties to match.

"You must be Lyle," Destiny said.

"Yes. And you must be Destiny?"

"The one and only. Come on in."

Destiny stepped aside as she opened the door more to welcome him in. Lyle stepped inside. Destiny closed the door behind him.

"This is for you, my dear," said Lyle, as he handed her the rose.

"Aww, how sweet. Thank you."

"You're more than welcome."

"Let me give you the tour. Here to the left is the bathroom."

Lyle peeked inside. The bathroom was dark and quiet, with the exception of a water leak coming from the sink. The stench of mold was overwhelming.

Destiny gently grabbed Lyle's hand and led him into the main room. The room was dimly lit by candlelight. To the left, there was a queen-sized bed against the wall. It was dressed in white sheets and a navy blue comforter with a gold star pattern. Each bedside table had three red candles burning. As the flames flickered across the white walls, an Apple Cinnamon scent flooded the airspace. There was a wooden dresser against the wall at the foot of the bed. It was painted black, with plenty of wear and tear. There were chips in every drawer and the paint was peeling all over. Atop the dresser was an old tube television. A rerun of a 70s game show played on mute. A mini fridge occupied the corner near the walkway, nearly hidden from the pile of clothes that were stacked on top of it.

"Nice place," said Lyle.

Destiny looked at him with a tight-lipped smile. "Don't lie to me, Lyle. I don't like liars. I know this place is a shithole."

"I'm sorry. I just. . ."

"It's okay," Destiny interrupted. "I forgive you. You get one free pass. That was it."

"Thank you. I'm sorry."

"Let's move on, shall we? What brings you here?" There was a brief silence—with the exception of static coming from the television. "Ya wanna fuck, right?"

"Um..." Lyle could feel the sweat accumulating in his palms.

"Don't be shy, sweetie," insisted Destiny. "I'll make it easy for you. It's eighty for fifteen. A hundred for a half hour. Two for the full hour. And five for the whole night."

Lyle took a deep breath and exhaled. "I would like to purchase an hour of your time," Lyle stated. "Full disclosure, though. . .I do have a fetish."

"Okay. I'm listening," Destiny replied, grinning as she awaited the reveal of said fetish.

"I'd like to handcuff you to the bedpost while I perform oral sex on you. Would that be okay?"

Destiny giggled uncontrollably, turning Lyle's sweaty palms into small ponds on each hand. "Sweetie, that's not a fetish. That's just a good time!" Destiny smiled wide, displaying a beautiful set of white teeth. "So, sure, but under one condition."

"Anything. . ." Lyle quickly retorted.

"I get to handcuff you first."

There was an awkward silence as Lyle immediately regretted his response. Almost anything. That's what he wished he'd have said instead. His anxiety had reached its peak and he began to sweat profusely. He used the back of his left hand to wipe the sweat from his brow. Recognizing his uneasiness, Destiny took two steps forward and placed her arms over Lyle's shoulders.

"If you wanna do it to me, I have to be able to do it to *you*," Destiny whispered. She leaned in and kissed Lyle softly on the lips. "What's right is right, baby."

Lyle reached in for another kiss, but was denied. Destiny grabbed his right hand instead and led him to the bed. He followed her to the edge of the mattress and continued to stand. She crouched down, unbuckling his belt as she licked her lips. She pulled on the legs of his pants and they fell to the floor. Destiny then proceeded to pull down his boxer briefs, revealing a fully erect penis. She engulfed it with her mouth. The warm sensation of her saliva caused Lyle to tilt his head backwards, his eyes closed as he moaned with delight. Destiny continued to perform fellacio on Lyle, triggering his left leg to twitch and jerk sporadically. His testicles began to pulsate as he resisted the urge to ejaculate. His left hand rested on the back of Destiny's head as she slid his penis completely down her throat one last time. She pressed her tongue upwards as she slowly released his phallus from the grip of her mouth.

"Don't stop," Lyle pleaded. He looked downward as Destiny used the back of her right hand to wipe the remaining saliva off of her lips. "Please?"

"I can't have you blowing your load just yet." Lyle sighed as he threw his head backwards with disappointment. "Don't be sad. The fun has just begun."

Destiny rose to her feet, smiling as she wrapped her arms around Lyle's waist and kissed his neck. Lyle lowered his head in an attempt to kiss her on the lips, but was once again rejected. She grabbed him by his polo top and slung him onto the bed. Removing the pants and briefs that had remained wrapped around his ankles, she discarded them to the floor. Lyle took off his shirt and threw it on the dresser.

He lied there admiring this spectacle of a woman as she began to undress herself. First came the bra, then the panties. She climbed onto the bed and gradually crawled toward Lyle. Her alluring figure became more and more captivating as she inched closer to Lyle. She mounted his pelvis, leaned down and planted a single kiss on his lips.

"Roll over, baby," whispered Destiny. The two made brief eye contact before he did as requested. He turned over onto his stomach, lying on the bed naked as the day he was born. The dark-haired beauty straddled his backside and proceeded to rub his shoulders. She moaned softly, rocking back and forth with each rub. Destiny leaned over to the left-side end table and retrieved two sets of handcuffs from the drawer. She cuffed each of Lyle's wrists to the bedposts one by one. Once secured, Destiny leaned down and whispered in Lyle's ear, "I'll be right back."

Destiny hopped off the bed and made her way across the room. Lyle watched from the bed as she scurried down the hall, eyes fixated on her plump buttocks. She disappeared into the bathroom, closing the door behind her.

Destiny quickly returned, carrying a square container covered by a thick maroon blanket in one arm. In her other hand was a black folded chair.

"What's that, beautiful?

"A chair," Destiny responded.

"No. . .the other thing."

"It's a surprise, baby. Just relax."

Destiny unfolded the chair next to the bed. She sat the covered container on the chair and made her way to each end table, blowing out all the candles. She stopped by the dresser and turned the TV volume up to the max.

"That's awfully loud, don't you think?" questioned Lyle.

"Something has to drown out the screams," replied a grinning Destiny.

"Wait—what?" asked a nervous Lyle.

Destiny chuckled as she mounted Lyle's backside. She leaned down near his ear and whispered, "I have a fetish, too."

Before Lyle could respond, Destiny uncovered the container, revealing two large rats in a cage. Destiny dropped the blanket onto the floor.

"What the hell's going on here, Destiny? Whatever it is, I don't like it."

"Shhh!"

Destiny reached under the bed and pulled out a metal bucket with a small blow torch inside of it. She sat the bucket on the bed, opened the cage and pulled out both rats by their tails.

"Uncuff me, Destiny! This isn't fun anymore! This is not what I paid for!"

"Lyle…"

"Yeah?"

"Shut the fuck up."

Destiny placed both rats onto Lyle's naked bottom and covered them with the bucket. She then activated the blow torch and turned the flame toward the bucket, slowly heating it up. The mouse screeches and scrapings layered over Lyle's screams like a fine symphony.

"Stop it!" screamed Lyle. "Why are you doing this to me?"

Destiny sat in silence, mesmerized by the flame delivering powerful heat to the metal. The game show audience cheered on TV as Lyle continued his attempt to break free of the handcuffs. He screamed and jerked more violently as the rats below him tore into his flesh.

"Noooooo," Lyle pleaded. "Get out!"

Destiny smiled as she could sense the rodents digging their way into Lyle's rectum. Lyle let out one more painful howl before fainting, no longer participating in the wicked game.

# HANDLED

## BY SHAWN BAKER & KEV NIVEK

Candles lit the room, accompanied by the hypnotic glow of a television. Transfixed, the man stared at the newscast, blindly stabbing his fork at an empty plate.

"...this is the third victim this weekend, leaving locals afraid to travel downtown at night. I spoke to police officials this afternoon—" The reporter was interrupted as the television abruptly went blank. The remote dropped with a clang on the dining room table. Startled, the man dropped his fork to the floor.

"Sir, if I may be so bold, what on earth has you so fixated on that television that you would scratch up the good China?" the bald butler asked as he bent over for the fork. He looked up as he rose, his face emphasizing his worry. He'd receive no response, as the man turned instead to his rocks glass, tilting it up until the whiskey was gone.

"Sir, let me refresh that for you." The call came from across the room as another bald butler equipped with a matching vest, tie, and goatee strode in from the hallway. He grabbed the glass and briskly moved to the bar, tending the glass as he spoke.

"What's the tension here? Did someone break more China?" Shooting a glance toward his brother, he received only a shrug in return. Walking back to the table, he sat the glass down and motioned to his twin. "I could use your help downstairs." He grabbed the plate from the table and headed for the hallway with his brother in tow, fork in hand.

Grabbing the remote, the man stood from the table as he powered up the screen. He immediately rewound the broadcast until he saw the familiar reporter. Pulling a sip from his whiskey glass, he pressed play.

". . .police officials this afternoon. When asked if this string of now eighteen homicides against our city's homeless population was the act of a serial killer, comment was declined. Back to you, Rich."

He tilt the glass once more, setting it down before heading to the hallway.

***

The sun beamed down relentlessly on the city streets as drivers attempted to beat the heat during evening rush hour. Those with air conditioning sat quietly in their cars in relief. Those without wiped sweat off of their faces while honking furiously at prolonged stoplights and fellow motorists.

New Knavish, Ohio was experiencing record temperatures this summer. Oscar was no stranger to the heat or the cold, for that matter. He had been a resident of the streets for the past twenty years or better. He never quite found his footing once his mother passed away. He was never any good in the romance department, so settling down with a woman was never in the plans for him. Oscar couldn't have cared less about a relationship. In fact, the only thing he ever cared about was when, where, and how he was going to get high. Oscar loved his booze, but he chose to rather smoke, shoot, or snort. He'd do just about anything he could get his hands on.

Standing on the corner of Cleveland and Morse road with a sign was never his style. He'd instead spend the time it took to make one looking for change in parking lots. Every day, he had a song-and-dance routine he'd been using since the late 90s. Members of the community he most frequently loitered in referred to him as "The Boogie Bum."

Oscar was having a good day so far. He had already made thirty-five dollars off of twelve cars, one of which gave him a ten-dollar bill. That's not including the good amount of change he found in the CVS parking lot. As Oscar stood basking in his glory, he noticed a black limo with a bald driver pull up in front of him. The back window rolled down and Oscar looked perplexed as he made eye contact with a middle-aged gentleman. The man in the stretch limo grinned at Oscar, amused by his blank stare.

"Don't stop the show on my account," says the man.

Oscar grinned back nervously, at a loss for words. Taking notice of Oscar's uneasiness, the man continued.

"No need to be shy, my friend. I'm here to help. I think I may have an opportunity for you to earn some income."

Oscar stared blankly in response. Then the man pressed on...

"I can provide you with further details, if you are interested. Just hop in and we can discuss it." Oscar looked in both directions before taking an uncertain step forward.

"What kind of work we talking?" Oscar stammered. He wanted any reason to say no, but he was desperate for a fix. The man responded patiently.

"I'd rather not discuss it here. I tell you what. . .jump on in, we'll grab some dinner, and I'll tell you all about it. No strings attached. If you aren't interested, hey, at least you got a hot 'n delicious meal out of it."

Oscar looked around for another moment, rubbing his fingers together nervously as he stepped up and reached for the door. It swung open before he could reach it, and Oscar timidly entered the limo.

# CRAWFORD DRIVE
## BY SHAWN BAKER & KEV NIVEK

The costume rack crashed to the floor. The sound of destruction woke Steve Benjamin from his daydream. Lifting himself from the counter, Steve made his way to the back of the store. As long as the shelving wasn't broken, this prick may have done him a favor. He was closing in a half hour and these costumes would end up in the clearance bin by Monday. As he reached the pile of unpurchased outfits, he could hear a maniacal, high-pitched laugh from inside it.

"Can I help you find anything?" Steve asked with a sigh. The shrieking banshee on his floor crawled her way out, entangled in plastic. Giggling into her hands, she stumbled forward, slamming into a table full of masks. She knocked half of the pile onto the floor as she steadied herself.

"I'm sorry." She hiccupped, covering her mouth. Steve gently took her by the arm, leading her to the front door. Swaying awkwardly in her heels, she held onto Steve firmly. He felt a twinge of guilt as he smiled.

"Don't worry about it, I was just about to lock up for the night. Here, take a seat, get some fresh air." He held the door open long enough for her to sit down on the concrete.

"Can you ca-call me an Uber? She hiccupped again. "My phone is dead, I think." She burped loudly and leaned into the nearby public trash can. Steve fumbled in his pocket for his phone. He pulled up the app and entered the store's address.

"What's your address?" Steve leaned forward as he asked.

"NKU Alpha Zeta house," she belched out in between heaves. Steve found the address and submitted the ride request.

"They'll be here in a few minutes," Steve informed her as he walked back into the store. He jumped back behind the counter to a glass-door cooler. The shrill ring of the store's phone caught him by surprise.

"Benji's Books & More, this is Steve. Hi, yes. We're actually closed for the evening. We are open from eleven to seven tomorrow. Uh-huh. No problem, thank you. Uh-huh. Have a good one. Happy Halloween." He grabbed two waters from the cooler's bottom shelf before heading back. Reaching the front door, he dropped the bottles in shock. The girl was gone, not a trace of her in sight.

"Hey! You okay?" He called out to the darkness. There was no answer. He looked around for a few minutes before remembering that he'd ordered the ride from his phone. Steve closed the door behind him as he pulled up the app once more. Before the page could load,

Steve was shocked by another crashing sound from the back of the store.

"How'd you make it all the way back here?" he wondered while jogging back to the costume section. "As much as I'd enjoy your company, I really need to close up now." Steve chuckled to himself as he looked around for evidence of his new friend's whereabouts. He stopped dead in his tracks when he saw who his visitor was.

A tall, ghostly figure stood amongst the masks with its back to Steve. Long grayed hair lay in tufts atop the shoulders. Leaning forward, it picked up a disgustingly realistic mask, the rubber made to look like skin with thick grey threads sewing the mouth of it shut. It looked too real. Steve didn't remember seeing that one on the shelf.

"Hey, buddy, sorry to be the bearer of bad news, but we're currently closed for the night. If you come on back tomorrow, that thing'll be on clearance." He nervously took a step back, inching his way to the silent alarm. The figure did not acknowledge Steve; it instead put the ghoulish mask on its face without turning around.

"I tell ya what. . .it's your lucky day. That's on the house—my treat. If you could just head out now, I can lock up. I'd really appreciate it." He grabbed the keys from behind the counter and turned back to face the creep. To his astonishment, there was nothing there. Steve stepped out from behind the counter slowly, grabbing a pair of scissors to defend himself.

"Okay, pal, time to go. You don't want me to call the campus cops up here. . .those bastards'll probably tase us both." His nervous chuckle was met with an eerie silence. "Come on, man, go get your jollies somewhere else! I've got enough going on without having to deal with this shit." He cautiously crept forward.

Out of nowhere, Steve was rocked by a flying fist. The crunch of his broken nose was followed instantly by a stream of blood that flowed into his mouth. Blind from the tears in his eyes, Steve grabbed his attacker by the hair, plunging the scissors into it with all his might. He heard a muffled grunt, but his attack did nothing to slow his attacker. The monster kneed him in the stomach several times before splintering his ribs with violent kicks. Steve lay in the fetal position, unable to move in any way to defend himself.

He felt his attacker straddling him, forcing him onto his back in the process. As the tears fell and his vision returned, Steve could finally see. Unkempt hair escaped the mask from all angles, the ghastly eyes staring at him black as night. The grotesque brute said nothing. It leaned forward intently while grabbing at the scissors buried in its shoulder, yanking it out with a twist. It drew in a deep breath under the mask, exhaling the smell of death into Steve's busted nostrils. It took another long sniff, as if breathing in the life that was steadily leaving Steve's body. In one fluid motion, it plunged the scissors into the side of his throat.

*❋*

"What up, y'all? It's ya boy Scootie Mac," said Scootie as he held his phone above his head, walking down a hallway. "We throwin' the sickest Halloween party in New Knavish tonight. If you're tryna get fucked up and have a good time, this is the place to be." Scootie adjusted his hat to make sure the bill was perfectly aligned with the back of his neck. "We got liquor, we got weed, and we got dope music. I just dropped a mixtape last week and that shit is fire."

Lenny, a short male with a scruffy beard walked out of a bedroom at the top of the stairs. He noticed Scootie going live on Facebook. "What about a party?"

"Don't worry about it, scrub!" Scootie replied as he headed down the stairs. "Don't mind that, dude. He might be here but that's only because he lives here. He won't be a problem, though. He'll probably be playing with his Pokémon cards in his room or sumthin.'"

"Fuck you, Scootie. I don't play Pokémon."

Scootie then walked into the kitchen, switching the camera view so the viewers could see the bevy of alcoholic beverages he lined up on the dining table. "Look at that, y'all! We got a wide range of delicious beverages. A little bit of everything over here. Bourbon, whiskey, rums and vodkas. And if liquor isn't your thing, we got a bucket of beers on ice as well." Scootie picked up a bottle of whiskey and raised it up toward the camera. "That's prolly what Imma be sipping on most of the night. I'm finna get twisted, ya dig?" Scootie set the bottle back down on the table. "Well, y'all have seen what we're working with on that front. Feel free to BYOB if you want. More the merrier. Party starts at eight. Two thirty-five Crawford Drive. Be here or be queer. PEACE!"

Scootie ended the livestream, sliding his cellphone into his pants pocket and making his way into the living room. Jayson, a tall and athletic built male was perched on the loveseat, watching a basketball game. "What the hell were you talking about, Scoot?" Jayson asked. Before Scootie could reply, Lenny walked down the stairs. "He was talking about throwing a party or some shit. He live-streamed it on Facebook."

"What the fuck, Scoot!" Jayson snapped. "You just gonna throw a party without asking either of us how we feel about it? What makes you think we're in the mood for a party?"

"Oh, so I'm the only one in this house who likes pussy? My bad. I was tryna be a friend and help us all get laid."

"Last time you *threw a party*, nothing but dudes showed up. Complete sausage fest," Lenny chimed in.

"Yeah, right. There were girls here!" Scootie replied defensively.

"Like two," Jayson responded. "And they were here with their boyfriends."

"You know what, y'all are so damn negative all the time. I'm Scootie fuckin' Mack, bro. Three-time New Knavish beer pong champion. I'm tryna help your dick, his dick, my dick. Everybody's dick! We're gonna drink and slide up in some lady guts. Y'all should be thanking me for setting up this opportunity. Instead, all you do is heckle me and belittle past events."

"This is bullshit," said Lenny, heading back upstairs.

"Fuck this. I need a cigarette," muttered Jayson. He grabbed his hoodie off the back of the recliner, putting it on before checking his pocket to make sure he had his cigarettes.

"Come on, Jayson. I expect this kind of resistance from Lenny, but you, bro? Don't be like that."

"You're an inconsiderate prick, Scoot."

"Jayson, it's Halloween, bro. What else were you gonna do tonight?"

"Fucking relax and not have to help co-host some *bullshit* party." Jason opened the front door and walked out onto the front porch, slamming the door behind him.

"Fine then! Be that way, scrub," yelled Scootie before walking back into the kitchen.

* * *

Standing on the porch in the dark, Jayson snatched his pack of cigarettes from his hoodie pocket. He popped one in his mouth but quickly realized he didn't have his lighter.

"Son of a..." Jayson stormed off the porch, going around the side of the house to the parking space in the back. He approached his white Dodge Dakota, opening the driver's side door and grabbing his lighter from the middle console. After slamming the door shut, he felt his phone vibrate in his pocket. Jayson retrieved his phone from his hoodie pocket and answered it as he walked back toward the front porch.

A masked figure emerged from the bushes behind the house, keeping their eyes locked on Jayson's movement. The creep gradually strolled toward the house, stopping once it reached Jayson's truck. It took a tire iron from the bed, observed it briefly, and then tightened its grip on the tool.

***

Jayson sat on the wooden porch railing, scrolling through his Facebook feed on his phone. He smoked a cigarette as he read through the comments on Scootie's livestream post. Giving the post an angry reaction, he backed out of the post. The front door swung open and Scootie popped his head out. "You really gonna angry-face my post, bro?"

"Go the fuck back in the house, Scoot. I'm tryna smoke this cig in peace."

"Have it your way, hater." Scoot shut the door, leaving Jayson alone once again. Jayson redirected his attention to his phone. As he exhaled the cigarette smoke, he was yanked off the porch railing and dragged to the ground.

"What the fuck?!" Jayson screamed at the masked figure hovering above him. The masked assailant raised the tire iron and whacked Jayson in the face. Blood and teeth showered the ground underneath him. Before

Jayson could  gather his thoughts, he received another hit to the head, causing him to fade to darkness. The concealed creep continued to bash Jayson's skull to a pulp, beating him even after he was dead.

***

"Bro, cover me," said Scootie into his headset as he played Call of Duty. "I'm about to catch this dude coming through the corridor." Scootie sat only inches away from the TV in a gaming chair, eyes glued to the screen. Scootie shot another player in the head, killing him instantly. "That's right, bitch. These scrubs don't want no smoke."

The front door slowly opened behind Scootie. In walked the masked figure, covered in blood. It shut the door behind it and watched Scootie with perplexity. "Yo, Carlos. You coming to my shindig, right?" The figure sneaked past Scootie and made its way up the stairs. "That's what's up, bro! Make sure you bring some baddies."

***

"Put ya money where yo mouth is, bitch." Lenny sang along to the groove blaring in his headphones. His roommates disliked this 'toilet karaoke' but hey, at least he wasn't throwing a party on short notice. Taking a drag from his vape pen, he set his phone down on the countertop. Steam flowed from the hot shower as he stood in front of the mirror.

"I need a trim job." Opening the medicine cabinet, he scanned the shelves in search of his trusty electric razor. The chaos presented within the cabinets took a moment to sort through, but he finally found it.

Starting on his neck beard, Lenny got halfway through before the power died. *Now, where is the charger for this thing?*

He opened the drawer under the sink, but found nothing there but an uncapped toothpaste and several used Q-tips. Dropping to his knees, Lenny tilted his head to peek below the sink. His head was nearly upside down when he spotted the chord. He slid his fingers behind the sink, pulling the charger up with him as he stood up quickly—too quickly. He was instantly dizzy, grabbing the front of the sink to maintain his balance. The world around him slowly stopped spinning, but something still didn't feel right.

Lenny felt an odd pressure on the back of his head. Before he could decipher what it was, his head was smashed against the sink. His right eye socket crushed by the faucet, he flailed in agony, trying in vain to fight off the hand that once again bounced his skull off the porcelain. Everything went numb. Lenny's limp body fell halfway into the bathtub. His legs felt useless as he struggled to pull himself up. A hand grabbed his throat, forcing his gaze upward. The long hair covered most of the hideous face, but the dead eyes were piercing.

The monster held up a bloody fist, clutching a toothbrush in it as he raised it above his head.

"No! *Please!* What did I—" Lenny fell silent as the toothbrush was plunged into his left eye.

***

Scootie stashed his controller and grabbed his phone from the charger. Making his way to the stairs, he checked himself in the camera, adjusting the tilt of his hat before tapping the Live button.

"What is up, people? It's t-minus ten until party time! Let's get this thing goin', y'all. Where's everybody at?

Pre-game is over; it's time for the real thing, party people." Scootie made his way up the stairs while shoulder-dancing in front of the camera. "Let's get it! Y'all ain't ready."

Reaching the top of the stairs, Scootie stopped halfway down the hall to dance for the people.

"Come on now, you ain't ready for this!" Scootie looked down at his screen mid-shoulder shimmy to see if he was getting any good reactions when he noticed something even better. In the camera view on his phone, Scootie could see the bathroom door open behind him. The steam floating from the door confirmed that Lenny was still in there. He knew Lenny would be pissed at him for this, but a pre-party prank could not only hype this party up right, but hell, Scootie may even be able to go viral off something like this. He would make it up to Lenny, as this was too good to pass up. He kept up the shimmy with a grin as he tiptoed to the door.

"You ain't ready, people. You don't have to get ready if you stay ready and my man Lenny is about to find out what happens when you don't stay ready!" Scootie pushed the door open slightly as he crept in for the big scare.

"Lenny! What's up, scrub!! You ain't ready for this, bro!" Scootie jumped up as he yelled, hoping to cause enough commotion to get Lenny to poke his head out of the curtain. This failed though, and as Scootie stood camera-ready, he was shocked that Lenny didn't react at all. He waited a minute longer, certain he hadn't failed to get a rise out of his friend.

"Lenny? Don't make me come in there, man." Scootie laughed as he set down his phone. "You okay, man? Look, I'm sorry, bro. . .I'll leave you alone. Just let me know you're cool in there." Scootie leaned in to take a peek behind the curtain.

"Lenny? Whoa. . .is that my toothbrush? WHAT THE FUCK?!? LENNY! LENNY!"

*** * ***

Scootie sprinted down the stairs with his phone on speaker.

"Nine one-one, what's your emergency?"

"Someone killed my roommate! I need help!" Scootie noticed Jayson wasn't in the living room. He opened the front door and checked the front porch. "JAYSON!" There was no sign of his friend. Stepping back inside, he locked the door behind him.

"Sir, what's your address?"

"It's uh..." Scootie lost his train of thought. He rushed toward the kitchen to lock the back door. "It's two thirty-five..." Scoot lost his voice as he entered the kitchen.  He was confronted by the presence of the masked killer.

"Sir, what's your address?" asked the operator yet again.

Scootie gasped and dropped his phone as the creature snatched him up by the neck and dunk his head into the ice bucket of beers on the dining table. Shards of broken beer bottle glass floated around the pail, some of them slicing Scootie's face. The mixture of melted ice, beer and blood invaded Scootie's facial orifices as he attempted to plead for help. The creature kept Scootie's head held underwater despite many efforts to break free.

"Sir, are you there? Sir..."

The masked killer released his grasp once Scootie became motionless. Scootie's lifeless body crashed to the floor. "Sir, we are sending help your way. Just hang in there. We will get..." The call was concluded by the masked murderer stomping the phone to pieces with its bloody, black boot.

# About the Authors

## Shawn Baker

 Shawn is an author, screenwriter, songwriter and podcast host. He's an Ohio native with Kentucky roots and a die-hard Las Vegas Raiders fan. When he's not writing works of fiction or cursing at referees, he enjoys traveling and spending time with the squad.

Twitter & IG: @bakerskreet

# Kev Nivek

Born in Knoxville, TN and hailing from Farmersburg, IN, Kev now spends his days working for the man in Columbus, OH. He moonlights as an author, editor, and podcast host. He can often be found hiking with his trusted ally, Knute dog.

Twitter & IG: kevnivek_